The Thing of It Is . . .

Also by William Goldman

The Temple of Gold
Your Turn To Curtsy, My Turn To Bow
Soldier in the Rain
Boys and Girls Together

The Thing of It Is . . .

WILLIAM GOLDMAN

Harcourt, Brace & World, Inc., New York

For my ladies

The Thing of It Is . . .

i

They almost had a blisterer in the taxi on the way to St. Paul's.

Amos had wanted to subway—he had spent ten secret minutes in their hotel suite going over and over his London maps until he felt maturely confident of guiding his wife and child safely from the Carlton Towers to the Cathedral. As they left the lobby Amos mentioned casually how it might be fun to take the tube. Lila, in reply, signaled for the doorman to signal for a taxi. On cue, Amos began his rebuttal, continuing until a glance down at Jessica made him fast shut his face: he and Lila both hated fighting in front of the child, something they had been doing much too much of lately.

They neither of them enjoyed combat, which made their increasing skirmishes all the more confusing to Amos. He himself, of course, was a happy coward, and Lila, though prone to bitchy things—an inheritance from her mother—was, at bottom, not unkind. Generally, when she was less than he would want her, there was some reason, and generally, if he had the time, Amos could come close to nailing it down. But now he was bewildered: they were in London; she was wearing what he thought was a new dress and had he been slightly more positive, would have mentioned how nice it looked on her. Her hair, of course, had been butchered atrociously yesterday, but Lila loved it, probably because Vidal Sassoon himself ran the slaughterhouse.

The doorman raised his right arm halfway, and instantly the lead car in the cab rank across the street jumped forward. Nervously, Amos noted the smoothness of the operation. Doormen, headwaiters, and Brooks Brothers salesmen all panicked him, and he groped in his pants pocket, he hoped unobtrusively, for an amount of change suitable to repaying the task of half raising an arm and producing a cab. The doorman turned and looked straight at Amos. "Yes sir?" the doorman said, and Amos inwardly heaved a sigh, because he knew the key to the code. 'Yes sir?' was 'destination?' and Amos immediately replied "St. Paul's Cathedral." With the hand that was not busy ferreting change, Amos began fishing through his various suit-coat pockets for the piece of scratch paper he had inserted upstairs. "I wrote the address down here somewhere," he explained. He was almost thirty-one years old and he had never, until three days before, been west of Chicago or east of New Haven, but he realized immediately as he said the words out loud that you didn't have to give the address to St. Paul's, that by even mentioning the possibility of giving it he had made himself suddenly a fool, and he hoped that Lila hadn't heard because as he stood there he was alone, alone in spite of the firm hold his daughter had on his pants legs, alone and, for the moment, vulnerable.

Lila pierced him then with an "Omigod he's gonna give the address."

Amos said nothing, but waited, head cocked to one side, wondering whether Lila was going to find the strength of character to be satisfied with her quick victory and shut up. She was an exceptionally pretty girl, pretty and sharply angled, without curves, and she looked, if anything, younger now than she did the night six years before when he'd proposed, managing somehow to force 'the thing of it is, I love you' past his lips. She had nodded and come strongly into his arms then, and Amos, standing and waiting beneath the canopy of the Carlton Towers Hotel, wondered what had become of her, his earlier Lila, wondered where she had gone.

"You'll have to forgive my husband," Lila explained to the doorman. "He's been in this country long disance."

Amos muttered what he hoped sounded like, "Just trying to be helpful."

"Don't you worry now," the doorman said, smiling first at Lila, then Amos, then down toward Jessica. "That's a fine-looking doll, miss," and he knelt, reaching out and patting the patched head of the rag doll Jessica held in the hand she wasn't using to grip her father's trousers.

Letting go for a moment, Jessica led the doll through the motions of a curtsy. Then she curtsied somberly herself. Then she grabbed hold of her father's trousers again.

The doorman repeated his smile and stood. "Charming young lady you've got there," he said to Amos.

Amos nodded, torn, because she was, in her own nutty way, charming, and strangers constantly applied the

5

word to her, which was kind and perceptive of them, but just once, one time before he died, Amos longed to have a stranger look at his child and say 'pretty' instead. But how could you call pretty a child who, Amos realized painfully, resembled no one else in this world as much as she did Edward G. Robinson.

"How old is she?" the doorman asked as the taxi pulled up. He opened the car door. "Three?"

From below, Jessica answered, "Four. I been three already." Then she got into the cab.

Amos followed his wife inside, first thrusting a handful of change on the doorman who, in turn, thrust it without a glance into his own pocket, saying gratefully 'thank you' and closing the door before informing the driver of the destination. As the cab pulled away from the hotel, they settled themselves, Amos and Lila by the windows, Jessica clutching Cuddly in the jump seat, facing them. After a moment, Amos realized the heat, so he leaned forward and pulled down the window all the way. It was a viciously hot morning, stunningly so, he imagined, for London. Amos didn't know how hot exactly, because the one person he'd asked, the inevitably German desk clerk, answered him in centigrade, but Amos imagined it was nearly ninety.

"Close it, huh?"

Amos looked at his wife. "I was about to ask you to open yours."

"*Amos*, my *hair*," Lila replied.

"Your hair is fine," Amos told her.

"That's because I paid Vidal Sassoon an arm and a leg

yesterday. Now if you'd like me to keep looking fine, close your window."

Amos reflected for a moment on how remarkably his wife, on occasion, emulated her mother. Amos hated his mother-in-law more than he had hated any living thing since Hitler. "It's hot," he said.

"I know it's hot, dumpling. That's why I didn't want to take the subway."

"If I close the window we'll be riding in a closed box and a closed box is just like the subway. And you wouldn't want that."

"Childish, my God," Lila said, and she slammed her window down, letting the hot wind blow through the taxi.

"Much better," Amos said. He assumed the skirmish was his and so was unprepared when Lila said, "How much did you tip the doorman?"

"What?"

"How much did you tip him?"

Amos shrugged. "Maybe a shilling, I don't know."

"You *don't* know; that's just what I'm getting at. You tipped the doorman probably a dollar's worth and you're such a hick you don't even know."

Jessica held her rag doll out in front of her with both hands, saying, "Cuddly wonders if you two would just stop it."

"I did like hell tip him a dollar," Amos said.

"How much then?" from Lila.

"Your back was to me—you were getting into the cab while I did it—so how the hell do you know I tipped him anything?"

"Listen—when a monetary transaction of that size takes place, just being in the vicinity is enough to—"

"A silver bullet!" Jessica cried. "Masked man? Why, he's gone." Then she cupped her hands to her mouth and went, "Hi-yo Silverrrr, awayyyyyyyyy."

Lila burst out laughing at the sudden performance and Amos smiled. A few months earlier, he would have laughed too—he had, after all, taught his daughter all the trivia she knew, drilling it into her from the moment she was first able to imitate his sounds. He had taught her this that she had just used, the ending to the *Lone Ranger*. And the opening to *The Shadow*. And Jack Armstrong's Hudson High song, and the one about Cream of Wheat they used to do on *Let's Pretend*.

These and many more he had force-fed her, and Jessica was really enormously winning as she charged through her various routines and Amos had preferred them to almost anything in this world until a few months earlier when he realized that she had taken to only doing her 'bits' when her parents were fighting, the nastier the battle, the longer the performance, her waif's logic perfectly clear and, to Amos now that he knew and understood, almost perfectly painful as well.

"I did give him too much," Amos muttered then. "The doorman. I don't even know how much too much. You're right. I'm sorry, Lila."

Lila nodded, started to say something, stopped. Amos settled back in silence. Lila joined him, lighting a cigarette, throwing it out almost immediately as the sparks from the hot wind made the butt unmanageable. Jessica began pointing quietly out to Cuddly various sights she recognized, mostly double-decker buses. The taxi moved quickly along Knightsbridge into Piccadilly, then cut down the Haymarket toward the Strand. Neither of the elders spoke until the taxi pulled up at a stop light alongside a convertible. The convertible's radio was on and 'Francie' was blaring into the steaming air.

"That song," Lila said then. "It's worse here than America."

Amos nodded. "And I thought the English had taste." Then they both sat quietly and listened.

Every few years, a song happens. Internationally. For no explicable reason, all over the Western world, one particular song is lionized to the point of agony. It becomes, like air, inescapable, and hiding from it is just as hard in Lille as in Kent as in Barcelona. One year it was the *Never on Sunday* song. Another year 'Volare.' More recently, 'Hello, Dolly!' This year it was 'Francie,' from the Broadway smash of the same name. Of the four, Amos liked the last one least, in spite of the fact that he had written it and stood to earn, from the song alone, close to half a million dollars. He never told people of his feelings toward the song because first of all, Amos never told anybody anything. But more than that, it would have screamed false modesty or sour grapes in reverse, whatever that might be called. It wasn't really a bad song—Amos had written, in his younger and more vulnerable days, an abundance of bad songs so he was not unfamiliar with the form—it just wasn't very good. The tune was weak on profile and the lyric, all about a young man who loved a young girl named Francie more than anything else in the world, not much better than pedestrian. Amos' original working title for the song was 'Which wouldja rather have?' and that was still the way the song shaped: a long question starting 'Which wouldja rather have' and then going into a specific of some kind, money or fame or health or life everlasting or Francie. And the answer to the question was always Francie. And whatever its faults, Amos admitted that the song was, God help him, 'catchy.' From the time of the first run-through it was the tune people whistled at intermission, and before the show returned from its out-of-town agonies 'Francie' was already fifth in the country as recorded by Andy Williams and zooming higher and when the show was open less than a month, six months ago now, it was number one in *Billboard, Cashbox,* and *Variety,* and *Time* magazine devoted a short essay to the song's phenomenal success in their Show Business section.

Lila loved it. She had never said as much in so many words, but there was a kind of look that crossed her face whenever she heard the song played publicly that, to Amos, could only indicate undying devotion. The success of the song proved, as nothing else in their marriage had, that Lila had not erred in picking a husband, that in spite of all the begging and wailing put forward by her mother, she had done good by sticking to her guns and marrying that poor Protestant from Princeton, Amos Mc-Cracken. This was, of course, Amos' own interpretation of what was going on in Lila's mind, and since it was all of his own imagining, he knew he had absolutely no right to get angry at Lila about it. Still, it galled him.

He was, in the first place, not from Princeton, he had merely gone to school there. If he was from anywhere at all it was Athens, Illinois, outside Chicago, a pit of a town to which he had not returned in thirteen years.

And in the second place, he wasn't poor. When Lila first met him, fresh as she was down from Wellesley, he was twenty-three and already making five figures a year writing jingles for TV commercials. He had his first Broadway show, *Blue Eyes,* when he was twenty-six. They had been married almost two years by then, and even though the show closed hideously in Philadelphia, a couple of the songs got recorded by top artists and one, 'Rachel's Dance,' he could legitimately call his first hit. After he recovered from the closing, Amos went back to work immediately, writing several industrial shows each year, so at no time did his income dip below thirty-five thousand per.

And he was a Jew.

Half a Jew, actually, his mother being the one cursed. 'Cursed' was really much too strong a word. Amos wasn't anti-Semitic. He just didn't care about it one way or the other, and as long as his secret was safe, he slept sound. He had every reason to: his hair was almost blond, he had blue eyes, a straight nose, and his last name was McCracken. He had neither friends nor acquaintances from his pre-Princeton days. His only relative, his late mother's spinster sister, lived in Tacoma, Washington; Amos had only seen her once, and that had been a Christmas visit over twenty years before. No one knew. Not his wife, not his child, not his anti-Semite mother-in-law, not his collaborator Donny Klein, not his producer, not any of the endless interviewers who had sought him out since the show's overpowering reception.

Amos never intended making a secret of his heritage. Things just worked out that way. His mother had run off with some salesman when he was still quite young, leaving him alone with his father. Mr. McCracken never much recovered from the shock of her departure. He was a reasonably unsuccessful accountant and he grew increasingly bitter as Amos aged. Alone, Amos suffered his father's spleen until the summer following graduation from high school when the old man died.

On the train to Princeton that fall, Amos swore never to return to Illinois. It really wasn't much of a vow: no one in Illinois cared.

Amos had graduated high in his class, with outstanding aptitude in music, and most colleges would have risked him. He chose Princeton because of the Triangle Show. He tried out for it as soon as he was eligible, and after getting his ego squashed for a while gradually worked his way into the organization. He wrote half the songs for the show his junior year, all but one song when he was a senior. He had by this time almost forgotten that he had a religion at all until one night senior year, when Cameron began telling some Jewish jokes after dinner at Cottage Club. At first, Amos flushed, praying no one would notice or ask why, praying Cameron would stop or switch to a different butt, or, all else failing, that someone else would silence him. But Cameron went on—his father was an insurance executive and he knew all the latest ones, clean and not so clean—and no one stopped him. A few people walked away from Cameron and Amos envied them. But then he started paying attention to what Cameron was saying. Cameron was a wonderful storyteller, his accent as good as Myron Cohen's; maybe better.

In five minutes, Amos was roaring.

So after that night, Amos had a secret. He'd had it, of course, for several years. But after that night he knew he had it. Once known, he promptly forgot the whole thing, except for two different times, the first when he was courting Lila. Mrs. Rowan put up enough of a stink that her daughter wanted to marry a *songwriter*, and if she'd known of Amos' mother's dereliction, Amos doubted severely that his marriage ever would have happened, no matter how deeply he and Lila loved each other.

And they did. Love each other. Deeply.

Then . . .

The second time he thought about it was when he told Marx. He'd barely been seeing the tiny man a month but he decided Marx ought to know, so as he lay on the couch, Amos tried finding some logical way of leading into it. There wasn't any, though, at least none he could ever see, and so, as the session ended and he was hurrying to the door he said, back turned, "Listen, my mother was a Jew."

"So was mine. Big deal," Marx said.

"No one knows is the thing."

"Then you're crazier than I thought," Marx said. "Don't feel so inferior about it. Remember: half a Jew is better than none."

As the taxi got to Fleet Street, traffic thickened. The heat, oppressive before, became next door to unbearable. They inched their way forward for a while, then came to an abrupt and complete and sudden stop. Amos began playing tunes on his knees. It was a maddening nervous habit of his, but unbreakable: at moments of stress of any kind, he began playing tunes on his knees, as if the caps were a keyboard.

" 'Yankee Doodle'?" Jessica asked.

Amos looked at his daughter.

"Is it or isn't it?" Jessica went on.

"Is it or isn't it what?"

"Are you playing 'Yankee Doodle' on your knee-caps? It looks like 'Yankee Doodle' from here."

"It doesn't either look like 'Yankee Doodle.' *This* is 'Yankee Doodle,' " Amos said, and he played it all the way through on his kneecaps. "You're a composer's child, can't you tell the difference?"

Jessica nodded.

"That's better," Amos told her.

" 'America the Beautiful,' " Jessica said.

Amos gave an enormous mock sigh. "I was playing 'Something to Remember You By' and I'm very disappointed in you, Johann."

"I was going to say that was what it was but Cuddly told me she was just positive it was 'Yankee Doodle' or 'America the Beautiful.' "

"How many times has it been proven that Cuddly is tone deaf? Really, Jerome, you must stick to your own guns."

"Play something else and I'll guess," Jessica said. She looked sternly at her rag doll. "You hush," she told it.

Amos began playing 'Twinkle Twinkle Little Star' with great concentration. Jessica hadn't missed on 'Twinkle

Twinkle Little Star' for over a year and she always took a very long time in guessing it, building slowly to her moment of triumph.

"That's a very tough one," Jessica said.

Amos nodded, continuing to play. "I'll give you one hint and that's all: it is *not* the national anthem of Bulgaria."

"You sure pick the hard ones," Jessica said.

"Give up, Jellybelly?"

Jessica stared at her father's fingers, doing her best to furrow her brow.

Amos looked away. There was very little about his daughter that didn't knock him out, but this look, this almost trancelike scrutiny momentarily affixed to her Edward G. Robinson face, was very close to being his favorite. So he looked away because if he didn't, he would have beamed like an overindulgent father and it was very important to him to keep his child as uncosseted as possible. The only thing Amos really didn't like about his child was his fault, not hers, and that was her name. Jessica. He loathed the syllables. Jessica was his mother-in-law's name and four years before, when his child was born and the name was suggested, he was too weak to fight. Besides, he thought that giving the old bitch a kind of nominal immortality might sweeten her up some. But she stayed as she had always been, a cold spoiled bigot, who took the name as all the cause she needed to become unreasonably possessive about her grandchild. Amos did his best to keep them apart, lest the harridan start to chill his child, and he retaliated about the name by never using it. He had not, for over three years, called his daughter Jessica. Any other word beginning with a J: fine. Jessica: never. When asked about his idiosyncrasy, Amos explained to his wife and her mother that he was merely trying to avoid confusion, which made a certain amount of logical sense if you didn't push it, and thus far, no one had.

"Great Scott, it's 'Twinkle Twinkle!' " Jessica cried.

"By George, the child's incredible." Amos reached out and shook her hand. Then he sat back in his seat and stared out the window.

In all this time, the taxi had not moved.

Amos closed his eyes for as long as he could, then opened them again, staring out. The taxi was stationed as before, permanently it seemed, between a W. H. Smith's bookstore on one side of the street and a shuttered pub on the other. Amos leaned forward abruptly and knocked on the taxi driver's glass cubicle. The driver slid the glass open. "Where's St. Paul's?" Amos asked.

The driver pointed straight ahead. "Up that way."

"Thanks," Amos said, and he sat back again.

The driver slid the glass shut.

Amos turned to his wife. "Wanna walk?"

"Walk?"

"It's the latest 'in' thing—you put one foot in front of the other and before you know it, you're walking. Everybody's doing it: Princess Margaret, Noel Coward—"

"What's got into you?"

"Well he said it was right up there." Amos pointed.

"What he said was, and I quote, 'Up that way.' What he didn't say was how *far* up that way it might be."

"I'll ask him," Amos said, starting to lean forward again.

"I don't want to walk," Lila said firmly.

Amos sat back and nodded. "You like it here."

Lila said nothing.

Amos turned to an imaginary figure in the empty jump seat. " 'Amos—how was your trip to London?' 'Listen, we had this terrific tour of Fleet Street!' "

"Never marry a composer," Lila said to her daughter. "If you have to, marry a dentist. But composers are a no-no."

"Daddy's a composer," Jessica said.

"Josephine, Josephine," Amos said, grabbing out a guidebook of London. "Do you know where we are? Do you? It's incredible." He flipped rapidly through his guidebook. "You see that store up ahead?"

Jessica squinted in the indicated direction.

"Listen to what it says about this—look—my hands are trembling with excitement—that store—that's the Sketchley dry cleaners that Dr. Sam Johnson used. Listen to what it says here. 'The Fleet Street Sketchley's is where Dr. Johnson had his underwear and boots dry-cleaned while at work on his famous dictionary.' "

"Oh I'm dying laughing," Lila said.

"You can't dry-clean boots," Jessica said. "You shine boots."

"Wait—wait—here's that very point answered," Amos said. " 'In the old days, the Sketchley had a special bootblack who shined boots while customers waited for their underwear.' "

"Oh," Jessica said, and she nodded.

17

"Migod," Amos said, clutching at his heart. "Look, Jackie—you see that drugstore?"

Jessica squinted around.

"That's the Boots Chemist where—catch this, it's history—where William Shakespeare bought his Nodoz while he was doing the final rewrites on *Hamlet*." Amos slammed the guidebook shut. "Oh, are we ever lucky there was a traffic jam."

"Pull your skirt down, Jessica," Lila said. "And sit straight in your seat."

"I was just trying to find the drugstore—"

"I said *sit straight*."

"That's right," Amos said. "Yell at the kid."

"When I yell, you'll know it."

"I still think we ought to walk," Amos said.

"Whatever for?" from Lila.

Amos was about to blow at that, because sometimes you just had to blow at Lila or go crazy, but with a final effort, he got control, smiled at Jessica, and started another tune on his kneecaps.

"Thank God we didn't take the subway," Lila said then.

"If we'd taken the tube we'd have been there."

"Or died of perspiration on the way."

"You're sweating like a pig now, love of my life!"

"Are you calling me a pig?"

"Gee, what a terrific idea—"

"Cuddly says for you to stop fighting," Jessica said.

"Tell Cuddly to mind her own bloody business," Lila answered.

"Please, Cuddly says."

Amos heard his daughter and he wanted to shut up but he was too far gone now, because back at the hotel when he'd suggested the tube she'd castrated him, Lila had, and he'd let it pass then, but now, in the heat in the traffic he couldn't, just couldn't, and before he knew it, the words were spoken: "Catch the 'bloody.' "

Lila whirled on her husband. "What'd you say?"

"I said," Amos replied, "that in just seventy-two bloody hours my bloody wife speaks bloody English like a bloody native."

"You said 'let's take the tube.' "

"So what?"

"You called it a tube."

"So do the English."

"They say 'bloody' too."

"There's a difference—"

"No!—There's none!—The only difference is that if you do something it's all right and if I do it it's not and I'm yelling now, Amos, can you tell?"

Amos was about to tell her, big, the words already forming cadences in his mind when suddenly Jessica was saying "Daddy, Daddy, Willie Mays got a homer today and I forgot to tell," and Amos, in reply, only flung his body at the taxi door until it opened and then he was gone, threading his way among the stalled cars to the sidewalk, where he stood, still, except for his drumming fingers, and all the time he thought Jesus Jesus take it easy you came here to save your marriage, not to kill it . . .

Until fairly recently, the thought of his marriage dying seemed as unlikely to Amos as his suddenly developing a fondness for his mother-in-law. There were very few things he knew in this world, but one of them was that he would never, no matter what the conditions, fuck up and split as his parents had done. Lila, he discovered on their second date, also came from a broken home, her father having been, apparently, one of those sweet ne'er-do-wells who from time to time for penance get involved with women like her mother. Mr. Rowan was a painter, or wanted to be, but Jessica cured him of that malady and set him on the righteous road of banking where he failed utterly, along with their marriage. This all happened when Lila was very young, and she saw her father infrequently after that, since he had moved back home to Nebraska and could afford, at most, only enormously intermittent trips to Fifth Avenue where Lila was, year by year, enlarging. Amos had never met Mr. Rowan, but from what he could gather, Lila's life was a death struggle pitting the sweet heredity of her father against her mommee's environment. From the very beginning, Amos knew that Mr. Rowan would win, although lately, more this calendar year than ever, he had begun to wonder.

He wondered about himself too: he had begun analysis in January, the week after *Francie* opened. The months preceding, he had felt vaguely discontented, but he put it all down to the upcoming musical. His first show's closing out of town had scarred and scared him, and this time things just had to be different. Donny Klein, his book writer, was always optimistic about *Francie;* not so Amos. Still, he worked very hard, in spite of the fact that his back began giving him trouble two weeks before rehearsals were to begin and he endured the entire out-of-town tryout in pain in an orthopedic girdle.

The day after the show opened in New York, Amos received fifty-four congratulatory phone calls. That night, as he for some reason suffered insomnia, it crossed his good mind that he didn't care about any of the two score fourteen people. An hour later, he admitted to himself that, wife and child excluded, he didn't really give much of a shit about any person, place, or thing, living or dead.

The next morning he woke Donny Klein to ask if his analyst had an analyst he could recommend. Two days later, Amos met Dr. Marx for the first time, their relationship continuing five mornings a week, from nine twenty to ten minutes after ten, Monday through Friday. Everything had gone well enough from then on, until the night a little over a week ago when he and Lila had had a blisterer over, as usual, nothing. This one terminated with her bursting into tears and running for the kitchen while he moved out to the terrace and began copying her boo-hoo sound with vicious skill. The kitchen window opened onto the terrace, and after a while Amos moved silently through the darkness and stared in, unnoticed, at his weeping wife. He watched her, appraised her, weighed her flaws and virtues carefully before deciding that he didn't give much of a shit about her either.

A moment later he was inside the kitchen, begging her forgiveness, holding her tightly in his frightened arms.

"What frightened you?" Dr. Marx wondered.

"Well, Jesus," Amos said. "How would you feel if you looked at your wife and decided you didn't care?"

"You want a divorce?"

"I don't know what I want."

Marx said nothing.

"I think maybe I want to go to Europe," Amos said.

"Alone?"

"No-no; with both of them."

"When?"

Amos shrugged. "Like maybe now."

Dr. Marx nodded.

"You don't think it's a good idea, do you?" Amos asked.

"That's for me to know and for you to find out."

Amos shook his head. "You're a comfort."

"You think Lila wants a divorce?"

"Are you kidding?" Amos sat up on the couch. "If she even guessed the word had crossed my head, she'd fall to pieces. I know Lila. She fights a lot, but at heart, she's a clinger." He shook his head again. "I don't know; why is it so hard, marriage?"

Dr. Marx went into his Viennese routine. "Vell I tell you. Dere was dis vamous chudge, unt he'd verked on dee bench for years. Unt dey asked him, 'Vy is it zoh hard? Vy zoh much divorzz?' Unt dis chudge, after zum sought, he zed unt I quode: 'It's just goddamned difficult for two people to live together.' "

On the sidewalk, Amos turned, and moved back into the traffic to the taxi. He stuck his head through the win-

22

dow. "Pardon me," he said to his daughter, "but I'm looking for a Miss J. for Jellohead McCracken."

"I'm Jellohead McCracken," Jessica answered.

Amos stuck his head farther through the window. "No," he said finally. "I'll admit the resemblance but this particular Jellohead McCracken never travels anywhere without her rag doll."

"Here's Cuddly," Jessica said, excited now, holding her rag doll high. "See? See?"

"Then you must be she. And I must be your father. And this must be my taxi." He got back inside and closed the door. "And this must be my wife."

"Nut," Lila said.

"Why did you go out there?" Jessica said.

"I had to relieve myself," Amos told her.

Then everybody, for all kinds of reasons, laughed.

And at last, they got to St. Paul's. "It's still standing," Amos said, as the taxi stopped by the front steps.

"Now now," Lila said getting out. "A truce is a truce."

"Can I pay the driver please?" Jessica said from the jump seat.

"Listen, Jerkhead; if I give you the money how do I know you're not gonna head for the border?"

"Please please please," Jessica said, bouncing up and down.

Amos squinted at the meter. Then he fumbled in his wallet for a bill. "Tell him to keep the change and see if he hits you."

Jessica handed the bill through the glass slit to the driver. "Keep the change," she said.

"Thank you," the driver said.

"He didn't hit me," Jessica said, and with that she got out of the cab ahead of her father. "I'm the leader," she said. "Where's Mommy?" She looked around. "There she is," and she pointed to Lila, on the top step by the entrance, her Minox camera in hand, taking the two of them as they started up toward her. "It's true about Willie Mays, Daddy. I read it with my very own eyes."

Amos nodded. Jessica couldn't exactly read, but since the summer before when she discovered her father's passion for Willie the Wonder, she'd pored carefully over the box scores every day. She could always spot Willie's team because San Francisco was the longest name in either league and after she found them, she looked for the letters HR. Once located, she was home, because 'Mays' was one of the words she recognized on sight, along with 'cat,' 'dog,' 'Kellogg's,' 'Sara Lee,' and 'Bumble Bee Tuna.'

"I sure hope he hits another homer tomorrow," Jessica went on.

"Me too," Amos said, and then they were up with Lila.

"Shall we?" Lila said, indicating the entrance.

"We've come a long way for this place," Amos told her, as they walked inside. "I just hope the food's all it's cracked up to be."

He had been so preoccupied with the heat and his child and his death struggles with his helpmate that St. Paul's ambushed him and as he stood stunned in the cool, quiet air he said, to his own surprise, "Aw." He had been in London for seventy-two hours and in that time he had slept to get accustomed to the time change, awakening groggily only to then sleep some more, and once reasonably refreshed, visited in no particular order, The Tower, Big Ben, and Westminster Abbey. He had been present for the changing of the guard at Buckingham Palace, holding Jessica on his shoulders for what seemed like hours so that she might see at least something over the crowd, and Amos' back began going in the process of taking her weight until it seemed to him almost a miracle that he had not doubled up in agonizing spasm. And he had seen the zoo in Regent's Park, the pelicans in St. James's, the crummy statue of Peter Pan that you need a compass to find, and the theatres on Shaftesbury Avenue and Piccadilly Circus and Soho and Trafalgar Square and number 10 Downing Street which, to Amos, was where Winnie lived, now and forever no matter what anyone said, and Marble Arch with the nuts spieling and Harrod's and Liberty's and Fortnum and Mason's not to mention an almost infinite number of taxis plus two wild trips on the tube plus seven rides with Jessica on the double-decker buses, only five of which counted because on the other two they had to sit on the bottom, and all the things he'd seen, he had liked.

But they weren't St. Paul's.

Amos knew, as he stood staring, almost nothing about the building. Wren he remembered vaguely, first name either Charles or Christopher, but that was all. He didn't know of Hawksmoor, like Wren a genius probably, and an architect in his own great right but content to serve here as clerk of works. Nor did Amos know of the gathering Wren made to flock to him for this most maximum of efforts, Bird and Mayne from England and others from other places: from Holland Grinling Gibbons and from France the great Tijou, who could embroider with iron.

"Can we see the Whispering Gallery?"

Amos looked down at his daughter.

"Can we?"

"What is it?"

"It's this place where you whisper. Mommy read it in that book you bought me. 'Don't fail to visit the Whispering Gallery,' it said. 'Under no conditions.' "

"That's what it said all right," Lila nodded. "Word for word."

"Okay," Amos said, and he started moving up the side aisle in the direction of the dome. About halfway there he passed a perfectly horrid picture by someone named Hunt and he was about to move on when he noticed the inscription underneath:

> *Behold I stand at the door and knock.*
> *If any man hear my voice, and open*
> *the door, I will come in to him and will*
> *sup with him and he with me.*

Amos moved on. When he stood under the dome he gazed up at it, head bent back, until he remembered that his orthopedic surgeon had said not to do that, so he moved to a chair and sat, mouth open at the rising splendors. High, high above he saw a railing, and occasionally tiny figures appeared, staring down and pointing, and Amos, like a child, waved up to them but no one saw.

Standing, he searched out Lila and Jessica near the Crypt entrance.

"What's down there?" Amos asked.

"Bodies," Lila told him and Amos paid and down they went, step by step, Jessica first because she had to be the leader these days, no matter where they were going. "I think Wellington's down here," Lila said. "And Nelson. Or maybe they're at Westminster. I can't remember."

As they entered the Crypt, Amos reached for his wife. "He's here," Amos whispered, pointing toward Wren's grave. "The man himself." Above Wren, an inscription ran. "Explain that," Amos said quietly.

Lila, the linguist in the family, replied, " *'Lector, si monumentum requiris circumspice.'* That's 'Reader, if you seek my monument, look around.' Something like that anyway." She moved off then, toward Wellington and Nelson.

Amos stayed with Wren. When it had become unshakably clear that 'Francie' was going to be the international plague of the year, Amos was able to see comfort in the fact that, if nothing else, he had, before the age of thirty-one, assured himself of being written up in the *New York Times'* obituaries. The *Times* was good to aging songwriters, and whenever a von Tiltzer or the like expired, Amos never failed to read every word. And no matter what happened to him in the future, he had written 'Francie' and as such the *Times* would remember him. He was, in a minuscule way, immortal, and 'Francie' was his monument.

Now, looking around him at Wren's, Amos despaired. He thought for no reason of Kretlow, his music publisher, and what Kretlow would say: 'Listen—don't gimme this Wren crap—what did he clear off the place? —tell me that—five'll getcha ten he didn't make a thousand off the whole church—*counting* kickbacks from the contractors.—Keep your Wren—just gimme Irving Berlin and I'll die happy.'

"It seems the boss has had her fill of the Crypt," Lila said from behind him.

"We're gonna see the Whispering Gallery and I'm the leader," Jessica said.

Amos turned around, far away.

Jessica headed for the Crypt steps, singing, to the tune of 'Merry Old Land of Oz': "Here we go and here we go and here oh here we go; and here we go and here we go and here oh here we go." It was a song of her own composition, her very first, and she sang it at any and all moments of transportation. "Come on," she called.

Amos and Lila followed her up to the main floor of the Cathedral. "I think it's right over this way," Lila said, moving toward the south aisle.

"How would it be if I just let the two of you go?" Amos said.

Jessica stopped dead. "You said we could go. 'Okay' you said."

"*You* can go, Jerome. You and your mother go and I'll just sit down here and gape like a tourist."

"But you said—"

"I'd really like to just sit awhile."

"You did promise her, Amos."

"You did—you did—"

Amos sighed.

"Does that mean you'll go?" Lila wondered.

Amos nodded. "But just for a little. I wanna sit under the dome awhile after."

"We're *all* going to the Whispering Gallery," Jessica said. "And I'm going to be the leader."

They went to the Gallery ticket booth. Amos paid and the three of them moved by the booth to the spiral staircase.

As they started up the staircase, Jessica said, "Daddy make up a song," so Amos sang, "We're off to the Whispering Gallery, for reddishes and sallery."

"That doesn't make sense," Jessica said.

"You didn't say you wanted it to make sense, Jerko." They continued to climb.

They moved slowly up the right side of the spiral staircase and whenever people walked by them on the way down Jessica always said "We're going to the Whispering Gallery."

"Where is it?" Amos asked.

"Up, evidently," Lila answered.

They kept climbing, but a bit slower now.

"I should've brought my Keds," Amos said.

They climbed on.

"Hey Jules," Amos called. "What exactly did your book say about the Whispering Gallery, do you remember?"

Jessica, half a dozen steps in the lead, called without stopping or turning: "It said 'When at St. Paul's, don't fail to visit the Whispering Gallery. Under no conditions.' "

"It didn't say where it was or anything, did it?" Amos asked.

Jessica turned around impatiently. "I've told you and told you and told you. You simply *must* learn to pay attention."

That was one of Lila's expressions and Amos laughed, in spite of the fact that now, for the first time, he began to feel occasional pain in the small of his back. "Squad, halt!" Amos said.

Lila kept on moving. "If I stop now I'll never start again," she said, and Jessica was moving too, so after a moment Amos hurried after them. He tried, as he walked, to peer up to the top of the spiral staircase.

It seemed infinite.

"It's like this is a Disneyland for sadists," Amos said, falling steadily behind his wife. The pain in his back was constant now, and for the first time his right leg began to ache. He rarely swore, and was even more rarely violent, but if his back could have had a life of its own, could have been an independent breathing thing, he would have killed it cheerfully, slowly, cursing it all the while.

It had gone on him for the first time on a Thursday morning while he was tying his shoes. By that evening he was bent, looked and felt aged, and the pain made movement impossible. The next morning X rays were taken and the result, the orthopedist assured him, was nothing serious: a thinned disc at the base of his spine which might, from time to time, cause pain but which, if properly cared for, would never need operating.

They measured him for a special girdle and he wore it with loathing for several months; it made him feel like a fag or a cripple or, on particularly grim days, both. Still he wore it, and it allowed him a certain mobility, and then, in February, four months ago, he took it off and had donned it intermittently since.

Lila hated the thing. In the beginning, she had been wonderfully tender about it, and had helped him move whenever she could, and had gone completely out of her way to allow Amos to avoid unnecessary movement. But once he had taken it off in February, once he was, for the moment, healed and free of pain, her attitude changed. And Amos had to admit the change was somewhat warranted, because, or so it seemed, every time his back had acted up since, it had done so prior to an occasion that Amos wasn't the least anxious to participate in, and Lila was. At first, Lila joked about it, but as the attacks went on, she began to predict them, and when she proved more than reasonably accurate, her hatred came. In her mind, it was in his mind, all the trouble, the whole of it psychosomatic. And Amos, at first enraged at her charge, came slowly to accept the unpleasant possibility that it might be true, which would have meant he was both crueler and more neurotic than he could cheerfully bear.

"Hey I'd really like taking five," Amos called out.

"An astronaut just went by," Lila answered down to him. "It can't be much more."

"I *mean* it," Amos said. The pain in his back was harder now, and his right leg was beginning to numb up, and something of this must have come out in his tone, because for the first time Lila stopped and stared at him.

"Oh?" Lila said.

Amos sat down heavily on the stone steps and crossed his right leg over his left, as he was supposed to do, and immediately the pain in his back lessened. Amos exhaled audibly.

"Daddy's collapsed," Lila said.

Out of sight, behind the spiral, Jessica said, "Come on, everybody, it might close any minute or something."

"Sit down, Jessica," Lila said.

"But—"

"Jessica—*sit*. Just stay right there. You can still be the leader. I don't want you getting any farther ahead." Lila waited a moment, then moved down to her husband and stood over him.

Amos waited for her to say something.

She didn't.

"It's my back," Amos muttered finally.

"Your back."

Amos nodded.

"Acting up, is it?"

Amos nodded again.

"Bad?"

"Depends what you mean by 'bad.' I'm not in spasm yet or anything, but it hurts."

"Hey everybody," Jessica called.

"Just a second, darling," Lila replied. "Well," she said to her husband.

"Well what?"

"Well are you going to come with us or go back down or just sit here on your ass?"

"I haven't formulated any plans, lovey. My back hurts, that's all, and I'm resting it."

32

From above them, Jessica sang: " 'We're off to the Whispering Gallery for reddishes and sallery.' "

Amos put his hands behind him, pressing the small of his back with his knuckles. "That really relieves the pressure," he said.

Lila said nothing.

"We're going to the Whispering Gallery everybody," Jessica said, and a moment later a dozen school children trooped by on their way down.

As soon as they were gone, Lila said, "Well, maybe you better just stay here and wait for us."

"Maybe."

"And rest your back."

Amos nodded.

"We'll pick you up again on the way down."

Amos nodded again.

Lila started walking up the spiral staircase. Amos stared at his shoes, listening to her footsteps on the stone.

"Amos?"

He turned toward her voice but as soon as he saw her he turned quickly away, frightened by her face.

"You're just such a stinking sissy sometimes I want to cry."

Amos sat quietly on the steps, listening as Jessica said, "Where's Daddy?" and Lila answered, "We'll meet him on the way back," before Jessica asked, "But what's the matter with Daddy?"—a perfect cue for Lila's "That is a question for the ages."

Alone, Amos continued to press his knuckles into the base of his spine. It really did feel good, whether it relieved the pressure or whatever it did, he felt better when he could jam his knuckles hard into the damaged disc area. But was it damaged? It had to be. Something showed up on the X rays and you couldn't make that happen from wish fulfillment. So the disc was bad, a weakness, a place that would flare up under pressure; some people had bad stomachs and some got migraines and he had a thinned disc so forget about it. "Ohhh, that feels good," Amos said out loud, as he increased the pressure from his knuckles.

Another group of school children paraded past him on their way down, chattering in their wonderful, silly accents. Amos watched them go, wondering what they thought of him, was he tired or a troublemaker or a drunk or a victim of amnesia suddenly plopped down somewhere on an endless staircase leading, supposedly, someplace. As the last of the children disappeared down around the bend of the spiral, Amos reflected that no one knew him like Lila knew him, not now or ever before or, he was willing to bet, ever again. 'Sissy' she had called him. Out of all the words in all the world, she had chosen to form those five letters with her pretty mouth. 'Sissy.' Not 'bastard.' Not 'rotten son of a bitch.' Sissy. It was incredible. To pluck from the world of the vulgate that one particular charge; it was stunning. No. Stunning was understatement. Stunning was—

"Are you all right?"

Amos looked up. Two elderly women were peering at him, pausing in their upward journey.

"You seem to be in some trouble," the second woman said.

"No," Amos said. "It's just . . . well, it's my back."

"Did you fall?" the first woman said.

"What a terrible place to tumble," the second woman said, more distressed even than her companion. "What can we do to help?"

Amos made a smile. "No-no, I didn't fall. It's just . . . I've got disc trouble, nothing really serious, but I've had it for a while now and sometimes when I climb I have to rest awhile and—" *What are you telling them for? Why? Why? You want them to mother you, you stinking sissy?* Amos laughed nervously. "Thank you, really, I'm fine, I am, top dollar as they say. Listen, I'll race you to the top, how's that?" and he laughed again.

"If you're sure you're all right," the second woman said.

"Thanks an awful lot for asking," Amos said. "See you now," and he sat still, smiling and waving at them as they glanced first at each other, then back at him before continuing up around the spiral until Amos was alone.

He slumped down on the stairs then, eyes closed, thinking of the word 'sissy' and what it conjured, of all the hated hours of piano lessons in short pants, all the taunts from all the other children, all the fly balls shied away from out of fear of his parents' reaction if he should just once hurt his hands, and suddenly Amos' eyes were open and full of tears because when he was very very young Joe D had hit in fifty-six straight, and if it had gone on much longer Amos' heart would have burst from the suspense since that was all he'd wanted to ever be, DiMaggio or Willie, taking off after flies at the bat crack, leaping impossibly up at the last impossible second and grabbing the goddam ball and whirling and

35

throwing dead on the line for the plate and slamming the old apple out of the park with preferably two down in the last of the ninth, and before he knew he was up, he was. Up and raging, taking the endless stairs two at a time, unmindful of the pain coming sharply from the small of his back. Amos bit his lip hard and continued to twist his way skyward, watching the stairs as he conquered them, keeping his eyes down, and then he shouldered his way past two ladies and they were behind him before he realized they were the pair who had been thoughtful, and it crossed his mind to shout 'excuse me' but by the time he'd decided to do it they were too far behind as he panted through the climb, up and up and still up toward the Whispering Gallery and then he was there. It was a circular walk the perimeter of the dome and halfway across was his wife and Amos cried "Lila" and as she whirled to face him he drove toward her, running with everything he had left and as he advanced she fell away from him, retreating in fear, and as he rushed at her he loved it that she was afraid and her panic only forced him to greater speed and then he was on her, his hands hard on her shoulders, shaking mercilessly while he spit the words at her, "Not again—never—as long as we live call me that you understand?—you call me a sissy again and I won't answer for it Lila and you better believe I mean it," and Lila tried cutting him off with an "Out of your head, you're crazy, crazy—" but he would have none of it, not now, and he shook her more fiercely, crying, "I mean it. Oh God, Lila, I never meant anything so much in my life and if you ever dream of calling me a sissy again I'll know and I'll come after you Lila, I swear—"

"THEY'RE HEARING!"

It was not just the size of his daughter's voice—he had heard her scream before—that made Amos stop. It was what he interpreted as the terror in her tone that brought him short. He looked at her, dropped his arms, and started to kneel beside her to tell her somehow it was all right but what she said next left him standing.

"Everybody can hear everything," Jessica said.

Amos looked around and as he did all he saw was faces, faces ringing the gallery, all staring at him, and as they stared he knew why it was called what it was, because suddenly he could hear everybody whispering about him as they continued to stare. He looked down away from their eyes to the floor of St. Paul's and he realized that he was now one of the tiny figures he had seen leaning over the railing when he was sitting far below. He had waved up to them then.

Nobody was waving at him now.

"Impossible—impossible—what's the matter with you people?" Amos heard and he looked up again to see a priest or a monk or some kind of religious figure in a robe hurrying fussily toward him shaking his head sternly.

"I'm . . ." Terribly sorry he was going to say, but the cleric would have none of it.

"You'll just all three have to leave," he said. "Now. Around that way, all the way around, that's right, now please, just go, we can't have this kind of behavior here, follow me."

So they followed the man, circling in front of all the others who were seated by the bench that ran around the wall and who stared at them as they went. This isn't me, Amos thought as he led his family away.

"If you'll just follow through that door and to the right you'll find the steps down," the man in the robes said.

Amos nodded dumbly and did as he was told.

At the top of the winding staircase he paused until Lila caught up with him. "Listen—" he began then, but she shook her head so sharply he shut up, wondering if she could tell from his face that he was the frightened one now.

They started down the stairs.

They went in silence, Jessica leading, then Lila, Amos bringing up the rear. They walked around and around, down the spiral now, and when they had gone what seemed an impossible time, Amos called "Hey, Jud?"

"What?" from Jessica.

"If I give you a message would you deliver it to what's-her-name?"

"You mean Mommy?"

"I mean Mommy."

"Don't," Lila said. "Just don't."

"Tell Mommy that—"

"*Don't!*"

Amos lapsed into silence.

"Hi-yo Silverrrr, awayyyyyyy," Jessica cried then, whirling around, facing her parents, then, in the unexpected silence, whirling away.

They continued on down.

Facing front, Jessica sang "Won't you tryyy Wheaties,

they're whole wheat with all of the bran. Won't you—"

"Shut up, Jessica," Lila said.

Jessica did as she was told.

The heat hit them hard as they left the Cathedral. Amos stood on the steps for a moment, blinking. From behind him, Lila said, "Well, are we gonna taxi or subway?"

Amos didn't bother turning around. "One thing about you, you just never give up."

"I was thinking of your back, Elvis, and how it might be easier sitting down."

"Look we were doing great not talking, let's continue doing great," Amos answered, burned at being called Elvis, a name Lila reserved for special occasions since two years before when Presley had recorded one of Amos' songs on an album, making Amos a good deal of money but hardly enriching anybody's soul. Besides, he was embarrassed: his back, although still troublesome, was considerably less painful to him now than before he had gone charging wildly up the stairs to the Whispering Gallery. Still, he massaged it tenderly as he moved down the steps toward a policeman. "Pardon me, sir, but how do you get to the subway?"

"Couldn't be simpler."

"Good."

The bobby pointed. "Just go through there to the bottom and then your first left and you're there."

"Thanks a lot," Amos said and he returned to his family. "Okay, let's hit it."

"Mmmmm, mmmmm, mmmmm," Jessica said, pointing to her lips.

"What?" Amos said.

"Mmmmm," Jessica said again, gesturing more sharply.

"Say what you wanna say, Jerko."

Frantically, Jessica shook her head, going "Mmmmm-mmmm."

From behind them, Lila said, "She locked her lips and threw away the key."

Amos looked at his daughter. "Yes?"

As frantically as she had shaken her head, Jessica nodded.

"Well it so happens I'm a master locksmith," Amos said, and he mimed taking a key from his pocket, inserting it between Jessica's lips, and turning it.

"Mmmmmmm!" Jessica said, desperately now.

Again from behind them, Lila: "That's the wrong key."

Jessica nodded again.

Amos took another key from his pocket and turned it between his daughter's lips.

"Can I be leader?" Jessica said then.

Amos gestured grandly with his right arm in the direction the policeman had pointed.

Jessica set off fast, her parents walking a pace apart, behind her. "Hold it," Amos said, when they were almost through St. Paul's churchyard. He looked around. "I don't see any hill."

"We don't want a hill, we want a subway station," Lila said.

"The policeman said it was at the bottom of a hill and if you don't mind, I'll get us there."

"Listen to stout Cortez."

"This way, Jerome," Amos said, and he took Jessica's hand, moving to the right, crossing through traffic to Watling Street. They moved along like that, hand in hand, with Lila considerably behind him.

"I don't see any subway trains, Daddy."

"You'd think he would have said 'Go to Watling Street.' " Amos quickened the pace, blinking the sweat from his eyes.

"I can't walk that fast, Daddy."

"Pardon me," Amos said, to a gentleman in a bowler hat. "But we're looking for the subway."

The gentleman pointed with his umbrella. "Just follow along Watling till Bread Street, then cross over first chance you get and go right and you're there."

"Thank you," Amos said.

"Can't miss it," the gentleman said. "Mansion House Station. Big as life."

"I'm looking for St. Paul's Station," Amos managed.

The gentleman took off his bowler and scratched his head. "Oh, St. *Paul's* Station. Well then you certainly don't want Bread Street." He pointed with his umbrella again. "Just go back on Watling Street the way you've come till you get to Change or Old Change, either one will do you, go right all the way to Cheapside, then left to the bottom and you're there."

"The bottom," Amos said.

"Now you've got it," the gentleman said and, smiling, he continued on his way.

Lila was up to them now. Amos said, "We're a little bit out of the way. We've got to go back. We'll be there in five minutes."

"Don't hold your breath," Lila said.

"Look," Amos said. "You wanna take a taxi, take a taxi. The midget and I are tube-ing. Want me to hail you a cab? Just say so."

"And miss this? Never."

"You're a blithe thing to have around, you know that? Birds sing around you. Flowers grow. C'mon Jezebel," and he took Jessica by the hand again, walking back down Watling Street. "Mommy and Daddy kid a lot with each other, y'understand?"

Jessica nodded her head.

They walked in silence then, turning at Old Change, going to Cheapside, taking a left as ordered, and there, more beautiful than any mirage, Amos saw the St. Paul's Station. Buying three tickets for Knightsbridge, he took Jessica's hand again down the escalator and followed the signs along until they reached the platform.

The heat was suffocating. They stood for a long time in total silence.

"Boy, this is some subway system the British have," Amos said finally. "It's really a fantastic thing. It's not like New York and that's for sure."

"Why isn't it like New York," Lila said.

"Lila will you just for once try—"

"Hot is hot," Lila said.

"Hell this isn't hot," Amos said, casually turning away, casually wiping his forehead with his coat sleeve.

"Where's the train?" Jessica wondered.

"She'll be coming right along," Amos answered. "Before you can say Jack Robinson, she'll be—"

"Jack Robinson," Lila began. "Jack Robinson, Jack Robinson, Jack Rob—"

Amos walked away down the platform. His back was aching again, badly, and he calculated as he walked, the possibility of his getting safely away with shoving Lila under the next train.

If there was a next train.

Amos looked up and down the track. Nothing. He glanced along the platform. They were practically the only ones there and Amos wondered briefly if somehow he had gotten himself onto an abandoned platform, by an abandoned track, waiting for a train that had departed many years before. No, he told himself. Cut the paranoia. There would have been signs. He walked back to his family. "I'll tell you one thing about London," he began. "It's the best marked city I've ever seen. I mean, in New York you can go ape trying to find Times Square."

No train.

"Tell you something else though," he hurried on. "When the British say 'bottom' they mean 'bottom' all right, but what they mean by 'bottom' and what we mean by 'bottom' ain't the same 'bottom.' "

Still no train.

"Make me a bottom song," Jessica said, so Amos sang, "When they say 'bottom,' you think you've got 'em; but don't make a bet, 'cause you're not there yet."

"That's very good, Daddy."

Amos bowed.

And the train came. Suddenly, with an echoing roar, and Jessica, surprised as it catapulted toward her, said, "Can I have Cuddly please?" to her mother.

"Give her Cuddly," Lila said, over the train noises.

"I haven't got her," Amos shouted.

"I really do need Cuddly," Jessica said.

"Don't kid now," Lila said, very loud, as the train slowed.

"I'm not," Amos said.

"Where's Cuddly?" Jessica said.

Amos and Lila just looked at each other.

"Where *is* she?" Jessica said as the train doors opened.

"Did she give her to you?" Amos said. "I don't think she ever gave her to me."

"She had her in the taxi," Lila said. "She was talking to her."

"Where did you leave her, baby?" Amos asked.

Jessica shook her head. "What are we gonna do?"

In answer, Amos lifted the child into his arms and onto the train. Lila followed, the doors slid shut, and Jessica burst into hysterical tears.

Amos knelt beside her. He had never been able to cope with crying and he felt particularly helpless now because of inexperience: Jessica wept rarely and Amos just didn't know what to do. He brought her to him and held her, kneeling in the middle of the car between the exit doors. Lila sat in the seat nearest to them, watching as Amos began to talk. "Now baby, come on . . . take it easy . . . that's the way, nice and easy, that's the girl . . . " Jessica's head was dead against his neck and he could feel her tears. She was crying harder than ever but Amos kept on talking optimistically. "Good girl, yes, sure you are, dry those tears, dry them good . . . " People were looking at him again, almost everyone in the car, and Amos raised his voice saying, "She's—" but he stopped when someone inside his head screamed *'It's none of their goddam business, let them think what they want, shut your fucking mouth'* and mercifully, Amos obeyed. "Now, now, it's not so bad," he said softly to his daughter's ear. "You've got lots of children." Jessica's crying had in no way let up and Amos wondered momentarily if your heart really could break no matter what the doctors might say and then he started talking again. "Lots of children, lots of nice children, lots of children just as nice as Cuddly and you know it. Some of them you even like more and that's the truth," which was a lie and he knew it when he said it. But then, desperate men do desperate things.

The dumpy-looking rag doll that came to be known by the hideous name of Cuddly (Jessica's one breach of taste, to Amos' mind) had come into their lives one snowy Manhattan morning several years before. They were still living on West End then, and Lila was nursing Jessica when the doorbell rang. Amos, who was finishing up the score of an industrial show for the National Milk Foundation, left his study, answered, signed the receipt, accepted the package postmarked Washington from the mailman. The brown paper was torn and badly tied and Amos opened it absent-mindedly, revealing a note and a rag doll. He read the note on the way back to his study.

Amos:

This friend of mine from Philadelphia sent me this clipping from an article in one of their Sunday papers. It was very old, the paper, but it said that you had written this musical show Blue Eyes and it was going to go to the Majestic Theatre in New York City after it finished up in Philadelphia and that you were married and soon to be a father. Well, give my love to your wife and tell her I hope I meet her some day and I made this rag doll for your baby. Well, it's been a long time, Amos, but I'm still like I was and I guess you are too. Good luck and all the best.

Your aunt
Mildred Rosenheim

It was remarkable, Amos reflected, how a funny-looking nine-letter name like Rosenheim, conjuring up nothing more lethal than a pudgy-faced soft-bellied woman unseen for so many years, could panic him so. Even as he was ripping up the note he was locking the study door, and a moment later he was kneeling in front of the fireplace, lit match in hand, hoping the kindling would take, and quickly, since this was an almost unused fireplace: his study was, under any and all conditions, Amos was willing to bet, the hottest room on West End Avenue. The kindling lit, bursting almost on command into flame, and Amos shoveled in the brown wrapping paper and ripped-up note and the string and was beginning to wonder if rag dolls burned when Lila was knocking on the study door. Amos crossed the room and unlocked it.

"You got a redhead or something?" Lila said, walking in.

"Just this here blonde," Amos replied, pulling his young wife to him, kissing her golden hair.

"Boy have we got a baby," Lila said as he held her. "One shot from the old boob and out like a light."

"My turn," Amos said, pulling at her blouse, lifting it, opening her nursing bra, kissing her breasts.

"What did you say your name was?" Lila asked softly.

"My friends call me Porfirio."

"You're all right, you know that, Porfirio?"

Amos kissed her breasts a final time and, after he kissed her mouth, he kissed her eyes. "You better get dressed," he whispered then. "If my wife finds us like this, we're cooked."

Lila began adjusting herself, then stopped. "You've got a fire going."

Amos nodded. "These Manhattan winters can get pretty rough."

Lila couldn't help laughing. "You are a great nut, Amos. You know what I think I love most about you? You are just so unpredictable. You are unpredictable and you are crazy and God help me, you are mine." She tucked her blouse inside her skirt. "What was the doorbell?"

Amos indicated the rag doll.

Lila examined it. "Looks homemade. Who from?"

"One of your infinite number of distant cousins, I expect."

"Didn't it say?"

Amos shook his head. "Nope. No return address and no note."

"I got some bright cousins, I'll tell you." She sighed. "Well, we'll find out eventually, I suppose. Someone will complain to Mother about how rude I am for not thanking and then we'll know."

"Then we'll know," Amos agreed.

If there was some question as to Cuddly's origin, there was none to Jessica's reaction. From the first, the doll became the child's constant companion, suffering with her all the early horrors, from weaning through toilet training. Lila, for her part, admitted, when pressed, a certain fondness for the doll, and Amos, once Jessica was old enough to eat out, often felt tempted to ask for a table for four when the three of them dined, something he actually did on Jessica's last birthday, when they all taxied out to Nathan's to stuff themselves in the back room on hot dogs and orange drink. "A table for four, please," Amos had said and Jessica's eyes reflected many things, none of them anger.

"I remember now that I didn't bring any of my children with me today," Jessica said on the elevator up to the suite. "And if I didn't bring them with me, that means they must be where I left them. And where I left them is by my bed. So that's where Cuddly is."

"Baby," Amos said, "she's gone. Don't raise your hopes like that. She's lost and that's it."

"Cathy and Susie I put at the foot of my bed and Cuddly on the pillow."

The elevator door opened and Jessica ran ahead of everyone down the hall to the door. When Amos unlocked it, she dashed into the living room where her bed was. When her parents approached she said, "I'm very mad at Cuddly because she went out for a walk all by herself and I told her to wait right here."

Lila glanced at her watch. It was a large, plain Timex and very accurate, though what she wanted, Amos suspected, more than anything else in the world was a gold watch with a gold band, something elegant and fine, although he never knew exactly where her taste ran on the matter. He had been planning to go with her to get one for a long time now, but somehow, they never managed quite to get around to it. "It's way past lunchtime," Lila said. "Let's have a feast."

"I'm not so much hungry as tired," Jessica said.

Amos looked at his not remotely fatigued child. "I'll draw the curtains," he said, and quickly set to the task. When the room was dark he said "Night" and walked into the bedroom, almost but not quite missing Jessica's whispered, "But he didn't even look for her," as he went.

In the bedroom, Amos moved to the window and stared for a while out at Cadogan Place, green and baking in the sun. Then he turned and made his way to the bed and stretched out. The bed was hard to begin with and he'd had a board put in besides, so as he lay still, his back felt, if not fine, then certainly better. Amos shut his eyes, and the sound of the connecting door closing did nothing to change him. "I've seen her chipperer," Lila said.

Amos grunted.

"Why didn't you look for her?"

"Look for who?"

"Oh Amos for Christ's sake don't be a half ass."

"Half-assed question, half-assed answer."

"I'm not gonna talk to you till you open your eyes."

"That a promise?"

"*Open your eyes,* Amos."

Amos waited, eyes closed.

"Amos, I mean it—"

"You didn't say please."

"*What's with you?*"

"I'm simply trying to forestall what's going to be clearly an unpleasant conversation. Can you blame me?"

"Please open your eyes."

Amos opened his eyes. "Yes, dear?"

"Please tell me why you didn't look for the doll."

"I'm tired of talking about the goddam doll and we haven't even started talking about it yet so just think how bushed I'm gonna be when we do talk about it so why don't we just do old Amos a favor and save his energy?"

"I understand the tack you're taking, hubby mine, because you've done it before. You're trying to get me so mad I'll be incoherent and then you'll win the argument. May I tell you I am not about to become incoherent this time?"

"*Jesus Lila there's ten million people in this town how the hell are we gonna find a rag doll?*"

"You didn't even try," Lila said softly.

Amos sat up on the bed. "Honey . . . use that mighty mind of yours a second, huh? We'd been waiting a year and a half for the lousy subway train and the temp was probably 50 C. and God knows what that is Fahrenheit and we'd been wandering around that part of the world over an hour and she didn't have the least idea where she'd left it and I'd almost killed you in the Whispering Gallery so what do you think would have happened if we'd tried retracing our steps back into the yummy sunshine? One of us would've ended up dead, Lila. And the kid would have screamed blue murder because she'd have gotten tireder and tireder and each time she'd have had her heart broken again when we didn't find the doll and better to do it at once and get it done. The doll is lost and lost dolls stay that way."

"You didn't even try, Amos. You could have at least tried."

"That's right, Lila. That's a really fine point you're making and I hope you keep on making it right through the summer into fall."

"Jessica asked me why you didn't even try and I didn't know what to say. Tell me what I should have said."

Amos spread his arms out wide and yelled, "Put in the nails for Christ sakes!"

Lila applauded lightly. "Now that the performance is over, perhaps we can get back to the subject at hand."

"The doll is lost, Lila. Gone. Bye-bye. Toodle-oo."

"You're not answering my question, Amos."

"The doll is lost, Lila. Isn't your mighty mind capable of absorbing that simple fact? Surely you've lost something in your lifetime. Try substituting Cuddly for what you lost and I'm sure my point will come clear."

"You're not answering my question, Amos."

Amos shook his head and started walking around the room.

"You're not answering my question, Amos."

"Where was I gonna look?—where?—Watling Street —you wanna tramp goddam Watling Street if we can

find it again and look for a rag doll eight inches high?—
you do?—then it's Bellevue for you, baby, 'cause you're
bonkers—the doll is gone. Where else?—Old Change?
—New Change?—the taxi?—You wanna do a replay of
our little farce in the Whispering—"

"The taxi, Amos!"

Amos looked at his wife.

"I got out first, remember? And then you two took a
while and I was on the steps and I took your picture?
I'm sure when I took it she didn't have the doll. I'm
positive Amos. I'll bet you anything she forgot and left it
in the cab."

"Lila, the doll is lost!"

"What did she do in the cab?"

"She wanted to pay the driver so I let her."

"And she put Cuddly down I bet and forgot to pick
her up and the mystery is solved."

"Nothing's solved, Lila, because the doll is l-o-s-t."

"I'll have those pictures devel—"

"Do what you goddam please but quit bugging me! So
what if you're right? There's a trillion cabs in London.
And maybe the driver saw it and took it home for his
kid. Or threw it out. Or the next passenger picked it up.
Or threw it out. Or any other goddam thing."

"Amos," Lila said. "Whether I'm right or not, there's
still one thing: you haven't answered my question: why
didn't you look for the doll?"

"I may be sober when next we meet," Amos said.
"And then again, I may not be," and he grabbed the bedroom door that opened onto the hallway and exited,
slamming the door all he had behind him. At the

elevator, he jammed his thumb against the 'down' button, and when the machine arrived he rode it to the lobby where he went directly to a phone booth, and after first ascertaining the number, dialed St. Paul's.

"I'd like the lost and found department please," Amos said.

A man said, "We don't have a formal lost and found department, but perhaps I can help you."

"Yessir. I think my kid—daughter—I think she lost a rag doll at the Cathedral this morning. About nine inches long. She looks like any other rag doll except her hands are sort of sewn together. That's the only distinguishing thing I can think of. She's what you call homemade so there's no label."

"Nothing's been turned in yet."

"Well she just lost it this morning so that doesn't prove anything."

"You're sure it was here? Perhaps in the tube while you were coming—"

"We taxied."

"That would be lucky for you then. There's a citywide lost and found for taxis. They're required by law to turn everything lost in."

"Where is it?"

"Perhaps you'd better ask a taxi driver."

"Yes sir," Amos said. "I will and thank you sir. I mean it."

"That's quite all right."

Amos hung up and hurried across the lobby and out into the heat. He moved past the doorman, heading for the taxi rank, and when he got there he asked the lead driver where the lost and found was.

"Lambeth Road," the driver said. "What'd you lose?"

"Nothing important. My kid. A doll. You know how kids are. She lost it this morning."

"Well you might try Lambeth Road tomorrow. Give it till the afternoon. If it's found, it should be there then."

"Great," Amos said, and after trying unsuccessfully to make the driver take half a crown, he returned to the lobby, bought the latest issue of *Time* and let it irritate him for what he thought was two drinks' worth of time. He had never been much of a drinker: he held it badly and the following morning it always hit him hard, but he couldn't tell Lila what he'd been doing because if anybody was gonna get Cuddly back it was gonna be him because when the divorce came, if it came, he wanted to be good and damn sure that Jessica knew who her friends were.

Braced for battle, he elevatored back to the suite and unlocked the bedroom door. Lila moved toward him.

"Are you bombed?"

Amos waved her away.

"You don't smell bombed."

"I had vodka."

"You never drink vodka. You hate vodka."

"I love vodka! I love all the things you think I hate! Because you don't know me, not who or what I am or—"

"I do. Stop it."

"I love vodka and turnips and cabbage and sweetbreads and hangovers and fighting with you and—"

"Please."

For the second time that day, a tone of voice stopped him and for a moment, mouth still open and ready, Amos stared at his wife.

"I didn't want to fight, Amos. I swear. While you were gone all I thought of was how we were going to make up and then we're fighting again and I started it this time. I didn't want to. I'm just so tired of fighting, Amos, please."

My God I think she means it, Amos thought. Then: maybe.

"Why do we fight so much, Amos?"

Amos shrugged, wary. "We don't fight so much."

"Only when we're awake."

Amos watched her. She was really, in her own stiff way, about as attractive as anyone he had ever seen. Part of it was her hair, he knew, being so pale blonde, and beautiful, except for when she let madmen like Sassoon or some other lovely get hold of it. And her skin was pale and her eyes were green and she knew how to dress. She still had on the green pastel summer silk she'd worn to the Cathedral and it caught the color of her eyes. She was flat in the chest, of course, and there really wasn't much behind to grab ahold of, but that didn't bother him often, even though he always thought, in his bachelor days, it was going to take some round-assed-big-boobed broad to snare him.

"Amos?"

"Here."

"I don't like fighting."

"Me too."

Lila nodded then and walked to the window, staring out at Cadogan Place. With her back to him, she said, "I'm sorry about the subway."

"Subway?"

"When we left the hotel this morning."

"What about it?"

"Don't you remember? You wanted to take the subway and I castrated you."

"How'd you do that?" Amos asked from across the room, his back touching the door, still wary.

Lila turned. "I got the doorman to get us a cab and I only did it because I was mad at you because, I don't know, I felt like I was getting cramps and my hair looks like hell—now don't try denying it, Amos, it does—"

"I didn't say a word."

"—and I bought this new dress just special for the trip and this was the first time I'd worn it and you didn't even notice—"

"I did, though. I thought it was beautiful."

"You could have at least grunted or something."

"I was trying to remember whether you transferred at Piccadilly Circus or Holborn—"

"That's what our trouble is, Amos. We're always thinking about the bloody transfers before the train's even left the station."

Amos nodded.

Lila began to cry, with no warning, and no sound.

They met in the middle of the room. "What'd I do this time?" Amos said.

She leaned her weight against him, burrowing for cover. "I just hate being a bitch, so. I hear the bitchiness

56

and I think of my mother and how she's gonna win out in the end and you've got to stop her, Amos. Everytime I say something bitchy, it's her and in the back of my mind I can see her nodding and smiling and saying 'That's the girl, that's my baby.' "

"How can you say such things about as fine a specimen as your mum? Why, when he let her out on loan, the director of the Smithsonian said to me—"

Lila started laughing.

"I cannot cope with laughing *and* crying. Choose one and stick to it."

"I choose you," Lila said, and her arms went around him so tight he thought his back was going to start hurting bad again.

Hey she's here folks. For a triumphal return engagement. Here she is: the girl I married.

They moved together to the bed and sat, and when they were safely down Lila turned her face toward him and then her tongue was stinging the inside of his mouth while his hands groped down toward her breasts and began massaging, which sometimes she didn't like because they were so small, her breasts, but now it was fine, just splendid, judging from her tongue's reaction, and Amos tried to visualize the new dress she had on and where did it undo, the front, the back, the side, and was it button or zipper and he had just about decided that it zippered down the back when Jessica either did or didn't make a sound in the next room. In any case, they both heard something and separated fast, Lila's hands moving instinctively to her golden hair. "What was it, you think?" she whispered.

"Beats the hell outta me but couldn't we give her a nickel and send her to the movies or something?"

Lila shook her head.

"Shit," Amos muttered.

Lila put her fingers to his lips. "We could pretend we were napping," she said softly. "At least we can hold each other that way." She flicked her hands at him. "Scoot a sec," and while Amos stood, she pulled off the bedspread, turned down the bed, then quickly crossed the room and drew the curtains. They undressed in silence, down to their underclothing. Lila slipped into bed first, Amos following, and when the sheet had them safely covered, he reached for her breasts again. "She's wide awake in there," Lila whispered. "We just can't take the chance."

Amos nodded, relaxed his hold.

"Don't let go of me," Lila said quickly. "Please."

Amos held her very close, wondering if he could possibly tell her the truth about what had happened that morning, wondering if it was safe.

"Oh-oh," Lila said in a moment. "You're thinking something."

Amos didn't bother to deny it.

"Well, either you'll tell me or you won't."

"The reason I'm hesitating is it involves him."

"Him?"

"You know."

"I can't imagine who you're talking about."

"If I tell, you've got to promise to behave. No tantrums, nothing. I mean it."

Lila snuggled up beside her husband. "Relax," she said. "Why should anything Harpo says irritate me?"

If Amos hated his mother-in-law, Lila loathed Amos' analyst. Dr. Marx, Amos realized, was an almost impossible figure to dislike, but Lila managed handsomely. Amos also realized it was all his fault, but there was nothing he could do about it now. When he first met Marx and started the daily visits, he felt, for what reason he knew not, compelled to tell Lila anything that happened that day he thought she might find interesting. Dr. Marx was a tiny man of forty-odd who had worked his way through New York University primarily by summer labor at Grossinger's in the Catskills. The moment he was able to afford it, he returned on the other side of the street, and vacationed there as often as possible, continuing his twin hobbies of punch lines and accents. He knew every punch line to every joke Amos had ever heard and his accents varied from excellent—Yiddish and German —to rank—Italian. He had the ghastly habit of ending most sessions with a joke of some kind and Amos, at first, felt obliged to roar hysterically whether he wanted to or not. One March morning, in the third month of treatment, however, Amos rebelled and said, right in the midst of Dr. Marx's recounting, "I've heard it already and it stinks." "Progress at last," the doctor replied, "thank God." As soon as he got home, Amos told that to Lila too, but she made no reaction.

Amos finally discovered her feelings in April. Earlier that day, toward the end of a particularly useless session, he suddenly shut his eyes and said, "It's just such a waste, my being here."

"Not as long as you pay me," Dr. Marx replied.

"Why don't you just tell me what's the matter with me. It would save so much goddam time."

"You really want me to?"

Amos nodded.

"All right, but you asked for it. Freud would have said this," and he began making German sounds: *"Zie haben der freulingerlungen."*

"Meaning?"

"You're fucked up."

"Why am I?"

"Think of my position. Suppose I told you. Suppose you got cured. Suppose I cured all my nuts. How're my kids going to eat, Amos? How's my wife going to get that second wig? I'd like to tell you, but you better figure it out for yourself. Don't sweat it though, kid: show me a normal artist and I'll eat him."

"He called me an artist, how about that?" Amos said later to Lila.

Lila said nothing.

Amos hurried ecstatically on. "He didn't call me a hack or a rotten crummy songwriter. An *artist*. Me. He called me that."

"He called you abnormal," Lila said then.

"No, honey; you're getting the emphasis wrong. What he said was—"

"He said you weren't normal. In my book that's the same as 'abnormal' and 'abnormal' in case you don't know it means 'unnatural.' He called you unnatural, Amos, so how the hell can you smile about it?"

"Honey—"

"He might just as well have come right out with it and called you queer."

"Lila, will you for pete's sake—"

"It just makes me sick! My God when I think of the money you're paying that shyster—"

"*Shyster?*"

"Quack, then. Call him what you want he's making a fool of you. I see it. Every damn day when you come back I see what he's doing and I wanna weep."

"Jesus, Lila, the next thing, you're gonna say: 'What do you tell him about me?' "

"Well what *do* you tell him about me? Nothing good, right? As far as he's concerned I'm probably some whore who's crushing your artistic soul."

"Where's all this coming from?"

"If you loved me, you wouldn't need any shrimp shyster analyst to turn you against your wife."

"How long you felt like this?"

"Too long."

"And you never told me? You repressed your—"

"—don't give me any of that 'repressed' crap—talk English—"

"—I don't know what to say—"

"—not knowing what to say has *never* been one of your problems—"

"—I've created a monster, for chrissakes—"

"—every time you say his name I feel like whoopsing—"

"—it has crossed my lippies for the last time, sister, believe me—"

He was almost as good as his word. Dr. Marx *was* mentioned again, but never first by Amos. Lila would make occasional inquiries as to his health: "How's Harpo? Harpo in the pink these days?" she'd ask when Amos was in a particularly neurotic mood. And he would do his best to answer softly, "Sweet of you to ask."

From the next room of the suite, Jessica knocked.

Amos looked at Lila, then sat up in bed. "Friend or foe?"

Jessica opened the door and walked a step in. She looked at the drawn curtains. "Are you napping too?"

"Giving it the old college try," Amos said.

"Well, my nap was going so good I wanted to tell you that I'd nap some more."

"What about lunch?" Lila asked.

"Maybe later when I wake up again."

"Just give a yell," Amos said.

Jessica nodded and went back to her room, closing the door behind her.

"She's been asleep like I have," Lila said.

Amos held his wife tight and started talking fast. "Okay, here's what happened this morning at the subway —I swear it's the truth so just try and understand is all I ask—please—see, a while ago, maybe a couple months now, I was on the couch talking to Marx and I was bragging on the kid—about how funny and bright and great she was and all the 'bits' she does and then I was remembering this piano recital—I was a kid and this horrible

teacher I had, she had her pupils give recitals every so
often so the parents could come and ooh and ahh and
think they weren't wasting their money—and I was the
prize pupil and last on the program and really scared
because the piece she had me down for I couldn't really
play—I knew the notes mostly but I couldn't play it so it
sounded like music if you know what I mean—and the
day of the recital I was out in the back yard playing
hardball catch with Howie from next door, Howie . . .
Howie Franks, Franklin, I can't remember, and I
caught a ball bad and sprained my thumb—well like my
folks went through the roof—here they were spending
their hard-earned you know what and I do a damn fool
thing like play hardball the morning of the recital and
then my mother says I did it on purpose and my father
says he's too stupid to do something like that on purpose
and my mother says no, he did it on purpose just as sure
as you're born and my father said like hell and whammo
—they're going to it, the both of them, hammer and tongs
over was it or wasn't it an accident and then—remember
I'm lying on the couch now spieling all this to Marx—
whammo I'm thinking about something else, about how
Jenny spilled her milk that time we rented the house in
the Hamptons for the summer—I was trying to make a
musical out of that Dickens book, whatever the hell it
was—I'm too dumb to choose *Oliver Twist—Bleak
House* I think was the name of it—and I couldn't break
its back, I couldn't make it work and the kid was in the
high chair having supper and I was storming around and
you said to knock it off and I said if you didn't shut up
I'd knock *you* off and whammo, we're starting into a

blisterer and she spilt her milk, remember?—she just slapped the whole goddam cup right onto the floor and made that fantastic puddle of milk on the floor and I said to Marx 'What the hell am I telling you this for?' and he said 'Beats me' and I said 'How did I get started?' and he said 'Wasn't it something about how wonderful your daughter is when she performs?' and right then I knew it all, Lila!—I saw it all so plain—she spilt the milk to stop us from fighting and she does her 'bits' to stop us from fighting and today that's why she lost Cuddly, to stop us from fighting, don't you see, she was so upset today—we got her so torn up that to make us stop she lost the thing she loves most in all the world and when she told me that, that Cuddly was gone, I just thought 'I gotta get outta here or kill myself because I'm not a bad guy, no, I'm a good guy, I am, and look what I'm doing, I'm killing my kid.' "

"Aw bullshit!" Lila exploded from the bed, jamming her way over Amos until she stood spread-legged and flat-footed on the floor.

Amos stared at her puny breasts, thinking only of Tania Snow, who played the second lead in *Francie* and had a body that never ended.

"She spilled the milk because she was one year old and that's what one-year-olds do, spill! As for Cuddly, she lost it because she lost it, period!"

"Always a pleasure dealing with a genuine sixteenth-century mind."

Lila grabbed wildly for her green dress, starting to throw it around her body. "I know you, Amos. Oh God do I know you—and I know in two minutes it was all gonna be my fault so I shut you up. You were just about to pin it all on me, Cuddly and every spill and every case of diarrhea and every cut and scrape, every goddam tear was gonna be my fault."

"It's everybody's fault, everybody's, that's the point—"

"I feel like a bloody zookeeper living with you, I swear. *What's happened to you, Amos? Where did you go?"* And she tore the door to Jessica's room open and disappeared.

Amos waited where he was.

When she returned she grabbed her bag. "Jessica wants to stay in. I'm going out. That means you've got to mind her, Amos. I'll be back sometime. Just promise me one thing: don't take anything out on the kid."

"You're a kind, sweet girl," Amos said. "I must remember that."

He remained in bed awhile after she'd gone, then reached for the phone and got room service. He ordered two club sandwiches and dill pickles and a side dish of mayonnaise and two Cokes, stipulating carefully that the waiter bring it to the bedroom door of the suite. Then he hung up, put on trousers and a shirt, and waited for the food. When it came he signed, tipped the waiter what he hoped was a reasonable amount, and when he was alone again, put the food down before going into his daughter's room. Jessica was lying on her bed, sucking her thumb. "You know what I'd like?" Amos said, seating himself alongside her.

"Hmm?"

"What I would really like more than practically anything would be a club sandwich with cold sliced chicken and nice crisp bacon and tomato and lettuce and lots of mayonnaise and a dill pickle on the side. Hey—that's your favorite food, isn't it, a club sandwich?"

Jessica nodded.

"Listen, tell you what, I'll make you one."

Jessica cocked her head to one side.

"Darn," Amos said then.

"What's the matter, Daddy?"

"Which suitcase did we stick the bacon in, I can't remember?"

"*Bac*on in the *suit*case?" Jessica took her thumb out of her mouth. "We don't have any bacon in any suitcase."

"Be quiet a sec, willya please, and let a man think. Now the sliced chicken's in your mother's plaid job, that much I remember. And the toast is in her make-up kit. Now if you were your mother, where would you stick the bacon?"

Jessica started giggling.

"I've got it, I've got it," Amos cried. "She put the bacon in my passport case. I remember distinctly her telling me now. Don't move, I'll be right back," and he got up from the bed and went to the doorway. Then he stopped. "I think we only packed Coke to drink. The ice is in my toilet article kit. I just hope it hasn't melted." Amos hurried into the bedroom, took the club sandwiches and spread them on Kleenex, tucked the Cokes under his arms, balanced two glasses filled with ice as best he could, and tottered back to where his daughter was. "Wouldn't you just know we'd forget plates?" he muttered, setting the food down on the desk. "Boy, wait'll I get my hands on your mother. C'mon." He patted the desk chair.

Jessica came over and sat down while Amos made himself comfortable on a corner of the desk and started wolfing down his sandwich.

"You didn't really make these," Jessica said. "You're teasing me."

"That's the thanks I get for bringing you a club sandwich all the way from America."

"But the bacon's all crispy and everything, Daddy."

"If you'd just once learn to pay attention to your father, you'd remember having heard him say that he kept the bacon in his *passport* case. And it just so happens that my passport case happens to contain, along with all its other pockets, a guaranteed, bona-fide one hundred per cent Hammacher Schlemmer approved bacon crisper." He finished the first half of his sandwich, swallowed some Coke, and started on the other half. A moment later that was gone and he wiped his mouth with the Kleenex. "Eat, baby," he said then.

"I am."

"You haven't taken one decent bite."

"It's very good, Daddy."

"Tell you what you need—a little serenade to help the old digestive juices," and he tore back into the bedroom, carefully opening the case to his silent keyboard. It had been a stunning gift from Donny Klein who appeared out of the blue at the airport three days before, lugging the thing with both arms. "This is only half the gift," Donny explained, and when Amos asked what the other half was, Donny said, "I'm paying the overweight," which he did and which amounted, all told, to a hundred and six dollars flat. Lila didn't know what a silent keyboard was so Amos explained that concert pianists used them when they toured, to keep in practice, and that they were piano keyboards, complete with keys and action and everything a regular piano had except sound. Amos had always wanted one but they cost too much and he played, he felt, too badly, to ever justify the acquisition.

Placing the keyboard on the desk across from Jessica's sandwich, he said in as drunken a voice as he could manage, "Play 'Melancholy Baby.' "

Jessica just smiled, picking at her food.

"Tell you what—I'll play, you guess," and Amos started 'Twinkle Twinkle Little Star.'

"I give up," Jessica said.

"You're not trying."

"Do you want the other half of my sandwich? It's very good."

"You could at least guess."

"I'm sorry," Jessica said.

"No need for sorrow," Amos cried, "because Big Daddy here has just got the idea of a decade," and he whirled to the phone and when the operator answered, said, "This is Amos McCracken in 1025, who would I see about getting a piano?"

"Daddy—"

"Hush, baby," he said. Then, into the phone: "That's right, a piano. You know, like with keys."

"I don't want to play piano, Daddy."

"It's your favorite thing, baby. You and me, four-hand duets. It'll be terrific."

"But—"

Amos raised his hand for quiet. "Is this the housekeeper? Hi. This is Mr. McCracken in 1025 and I have this sudden crying need for a piano and I guess you're the lady that might get one for me. Now I don't care what kind—upright, spinet, baby grand, whatever you've got's just fine."

"I won't play."

"One sec," Amos said into the phone. He put his hand over the mouthpiece. "Of course you'll play, now quit being overdramatic. At home you're always begging me to play piano with you. Right? Is that right? Yes or no. *Tell me!*"

"Don't yell at me like that, Daddy."

"Nobody's yelling, but you're getting awfully damn sensitive in your old age if you ask me."

"I'm not, I'm not, I just don't wanna play any piano, that's all."

"What do you wanna do?"

"Nap."

"You've *been* napping."

"Daddy—"

"Just one sec, Mrs. Housekeeper, and I'll get everything straightened away up here. Sorry to keep you waiting." He put his hand over the mouthpiece again. "All right now, what's it gonna be, yes or no?"

Jessica shook her head.

"Terribly sorry to bother you," Amos said into the

phone. "It seems it wasn't a piano I needed, it was a doodlesack. You wouldn't happen to have one of those lying around? No? Well, that's the way the ball bounces. Thanks a lot anyway." He hung up and marched without a word to the desk where he picked up his silent keyboard, being careful to first bend his knees so as not to send his back into spasm. He lugged the keyboard back into the bedroom, kicking the door shut with all he had so that the slamming sound nearly startled him and he *knew* it was coming, then carefully put the keyboard back into its case. Locking the case, he blew on his fingers a moment, then whirled, starting back toward his daughter, readying a lecture on how spoiled brats were not exactly the most sought-after objects in this world when scorn bubbled through his brain carrying with it the message: You committable prick, she's *four!*

Amos sagged and, turning weary and numb from his beloved's room, crossed to the desk, opened it, grabbed for a sheet of paper, got it the second grab, and scrawled a message thereon: 'They are keeping me prisoner in here so whoever you are, tell J. Edgar Hoover.' He had the paper already folded before remembering that Jessica couldn't read it so he tore it up and filled another sheet of paper with very large printed letters that read, 'I am crazy for you.' Strictly speaking, Jessica wouldn't be able to read this either, but he had sent her the message so many times from so many places that he knew she would recognize the meaning. Folding the paper, he inserted it in an envelope and walked back to the adjoining door, got slowly to his knees, and slipped the paper as noisily as possible underneath, leaving enough of it on his side so that he would know when the message was received.

It was received almost immediately, and Amos lay down on the rug until a reply came. He figured he would either get a page full of stars or a page full of X's, but the odds favored stars. There was an outside chance he might get nothing but J's, since she had recently learned how to make them recognizably. Or possibly a big face smoking a pipe, the kid's image of a father, or a family portrait, consisting of one large stick figure—the kid herself—plus two small—him and Lila.

He got: nothing. Zero. Zilch. Nada. Nil. Void. Amos waited and waited, praying only that if Lila arrived suddenly, God would gift him with wit enough to figure some reasonable explanation covering why a grown man should be lying on the floor, one eye closed, peering under a door. But Lila didn't surprise him and eventually Amos decided he was a major league fool, lying there, so holding out only a while longer, he got to his feet and crossed to the bed, lying on its hard surface, giving a little groan of pleasure as spine and mattress connected.

His back had begun to hurt him.

Lila got in a little before six and on the hour precisely Mrs. Piper, the Mary-Poppins-type nanny from Universal Aunts, arrived, as she had the previous two evenings. Jessica seemed glad enough to see her, and Lila, after playing a few minutes with her daughter, prepared to get dressed. It was asking for trouble, Amos realized, going out with Lila alone, but they had managed to get tickets for Olivier's *Othello* at the National Theatre and when you got a chance to see Sir Larry in the flesh, you went.

So they left, Lila being ready on time for a change, which for some reason irritated Amos more than her usual tardiness ever would have done. They taxied to the theatre, keeping conversation to a remarkable minimum, and they saw the show, and Amos found the whole thing enormously depressing. Not the not talking; he had gotten used to that lately. It was Sir Larry that gloomed him. Not just the man alone; the whole experience. It was all so goddam wonderful, and if you're American, and you really love the theatre, and Amos did, it was like loving the New York Mets: sometimes you scored but mostly you just sat there and ate it. And Amos, in the taxi back to the Carlton Towers, couldn't get the American National Theatre out of his head: he had seen their productions, all of them from the beginning, and each and every time he'd wanted to cup his hands over his mouth and yell 'Stop the fight' they were that bad. And tonight it had all seemed so easy, such fun, and that was really the name of the game, fun, entertainment, call it what you will. Fun meant merriment and merriment meant joy and that was what he'd seen tonight, a little joy up there, nice and easy, no sweat about it, and Amos had wept toward the ending for the Moor like he hadn't wept since Cervantes had brought Don Quixote down.

Lila ordered roast beef back at the hotel dining room and Amos had the same. They ate in silence, then made their way to the suite. Mrs. Piper reported that all had gone well, if a trifle quietly, and Amos paid and blessed her and said he'd see her tomorrow, same time, same station. Then he went in to look at his sleeping beauty. Lila, already there, exited as he entered, and Amos stared for a long time down at his creature, smoothing the hair away from her Edward G. Robinson face. She stirred, so he quickly left, closing the door behind him.

Lila was already in her nightgown, seated in front of the mirror by the dressing table, wiping the crap off her face. Amos washed, got naked, and climbed into the sack. Lila turned out the lights and opened the curtains leading to the terrace. Hot moonlight framed her and Amos examined her scrawny body as best he could. He felt no desire whatsoever, but they couldn't go on like this, not much longer anyway, not and both stay alive, so he left the bed, he hoped gracefully, and took Lila in his arms and kissed her, he hoped passionately, his hands roving.

"I'm getting the curse I think," she said, and broke his grip, climbing into bed.

Amos just stood there, momentarily staggered at the amount of vitriol he suddenly felt blistering his body. He reached out with his arms, embracing air, kissing it, whispering, "Oh Lila, Lila, God I love holding you."

Lila said nothing.

Still holding his arms out, naked Amos began to waltz through the darkened room. "You're like a feather, my sweetness," he whispered, whirling around and around.

"You're gonna crack your skull like that," Lila warned.

"Make me immortal with a smack on the lippies," Amos whispered, bending slightly forward, making an enormous kissing sound.

"After you're wounded, just don't come to me for sympathy."

Amos kept on dancing.

"Amos, it's late."

"You're right." He stopped dancing. "And we've got a big day tomorrow."

"What's tomorrow?" Lila asked.

Amos got into bed before answering. "The tournament." He lay very still, staring at the ceiling, being very careful to stay away from his wife, on his own side of the bed.

"I'm not going to ask what tournament. Good night, Amos."

"It's the finals of the International Gushing Championship. You're among the favorites."

"I said good night, Amos."

"Sometimes I really think you're a hemophiliac, Lila."

"Just go to hell."

"I'm serious. You're the only girl in the continent of North America that has a twenty-eight-day cycle in reverse. Bleed twenty-three days, then five days off."

"You're such a tasteless—"

"Well it's true. I mean Jesus, either you've got the curse or you're getting it or you think you're about to get it or you've just gotten over it or you're smack in the middle between bleeds and that renders you *hors de combat* or—"

"Shut your fat face!"

"I'm just showing a little husbandly concern, Lila.

74

How do you think it'd look in the papers: 'Composer's wife bleeds to death.' "

"God damn you!—"

"I really think the Gushing Championship is as good as yours, Lila, only—"

"I won't spend the night in the same room with you!"

"Same here, baby!" and Amos was out of bed first, groping for his clothes. He dressed wildly, then left the room for downstairs. In the bar, he made discreet arrangements for a bottle of Scotch and, the purchase under his arm, returned to the suite, entering the bedroom only long enough to grab the silent keyboard from its case. Lila was, to his surprise, weeping and, he wasn't quite sure how he felt about that, but before he'd decided, he was on the terrace overlooking Cadogan Place, the silent keyboard spread before him in the moonlight. Amos sat and took a long swallow of Scotch. It was terrific whisky, the best, and it probably would have gone down easier if he had ever had a stomach for the stuff, but as soon as his throat stopped burning, he gamely took another, longer swallow.

Then he began to play.

He pounded down on the keyboard with all the power of his strong fingers, pausing only for more Scotch, and Cadogan Place was lovely in the moonlight. Shut on his silent terrace, with his silent keyboard, Amos played, wondering why he had been so cruel to Lila, wondering what her stunned reaction would be if she ever dreamed he was so seriously contemplating leaving her, but then, as he managed a particularly magnificent arpeggio he understood the trivia of it all, the overpowering insignificance, because, Amos realized, the Scotch bottle half gone, that he was like Beethoven! making music for all but him to hear, and if you were Beethoven! then nothing could bother you but your art and he was that, an artist, Marx had said so, so on he played, with occasional sips for refreshment, and nothing bothered him, Ludwig van Amos Beethoven!—not the moonlight, not the fading stars, not a brief flicking shower, not the morning sun.

The note was undecipherable. Lila's handwriting was as big and bold as ever, it was Amos's eyes that made everything code. He staggered toward the bathroom and buried his head under the shower. He had not had too much to drink since the night *Francie* opened, and then he was only high. Amos turned off the shower and went back to the desk where the note was. The words eventually came into focus:

Amos:
You smell like a brewery. I have kept Jessica away from you as much as I could and we are now off to Battersea Park for at least through lunch. Try and be civilized on our return.
                                                                L.

Amos steamed. The bitch. The rotten goddam bitch. She hated amusement parks, old bitch Lila did, and she was only going to Battersea now because she was trying to make points with the kid. He, *Amos*, was the one that was going to take her to Battersea Park. He had promised, pledged, sworn, and now the titless wonder had stolen his day.

The effort of anger exhausted him and Amos slumped down in the desk chair trying to clear the fog. When he was able, he made his way along the walls to the bathroom and turned on the shower full and sat in the tub letting the water cascade over his head. With both hands, he tried to fumble the stopper into the drain and when it looked like he couldn't do it he realized it was because it didn't fit, the stopper was the wrong size, something Lila had undoubtedly seen to, making the change before her departure, switching a huge stopper for one the proper size so that Amos would go mad trying to slip the one into the other.

But at last he triumphed and then he just sat straight, the water thudding against his skull, the tub slowly filling all the way up to the top. When it was full, Amos lay back, water sloshing over the tub sides onto the tile. He would have stayed for an even longer time like that if he hadn't been seized with a paranoid fear of drowning. Amos stood, grabbed a towel, dried his body. Then he squinted at his watch, saw that it was already close to twelve and that spurred him into dressing quickly, scrawling a note of his own: 'Off shopping,' and then making his way out of the hotel where he took the tube to St. Paul's Cathedral.

Inside it was again cool, and Amos asked the lady selling mementos where the lost and found department might be, or whatever there was that passed as a lost and found department. She directed him down the south aisle almost all the way, to a door marked 'Private.' Amos knocked but there was no answer. He knocked again, louder, when a passing cleric stopped. "May I be of some assistance, sir?"

"I'm looking for the lost and found. I was told it was in here."

"That's quite right, sir, but there'll be no one back till after lunch."

"When will that be?"

"I should think no later than half past one, sir."

Amos looked at his watch. "Thanks," he said. "Thank you." The cleric nodded and walked away as Amos wondered how he was going to pass fifty-five minutes without going mad. He decided to put a little something in his stomach but on his way to the exit door he walked by the painting he had seen the day before.

> *Behold I stand at the door and knock.*
> *If any man hear my voice, and open*
> *the door, I will come in to him and will*
> *sup with him and he with me.*

Damn that's pretty, Amos thought, taking a chair, staring at the inscription, wondering what the hell it meant. He tried puzzling at it, but his mind wasn't up to much, and after deciding that his stomach wasn't up to much either, Amos slumped in the chair and stared at the inscription and the simple picture of, he guessed, Jesus or somebody, above it.

At one twenty-nine Amos went back to the door marked 'Private.' This time when he banged, a cleric peered out at him. "You wanted something, sir?"

"I'm sorry to bother you, father, but my daughter I think lost a doll here yesterday."

"A rag doll?"

"Oh you found it, thank God," Amos said, reaching out stupidly to shake the other man's hand. "Listen, you don't know how much easier my life's gonna be."

The other man flushed. "I'm terribly sorry—it hasn't been found at all—you see, I was the one you spoke to on the phone. Yesterday afternoon."

"Listen," Amos said. "It wasn't important."

"You're welcome to look, but nothing's come in at all like a rag doll."

"You wouldn't mind?"

The cleric gestured and Amos walked through the door. The cleric stopped and pointed to a series of shelves behind the door. "We keep everything here."

"Thanks anyway," Amos said after a moment's looking at the barren shelves.

"Have you tried the taxi lost and found? If she lost it in the taxi there's a very strong chance of its being there."

"I'm on my way sir," Amos said, smiling, giving a little wave, making his way quickly out of the building. He wasn't really disappointed at not finding it here, because he knew the odds just weren't good, and he could have gone to the taxi place first, which would have been the logical thing to do except Lila had said it would be at the taxi place so he had hoped against hope for the Cathedral.

On the Cathedral steps, Amos paused a moment at the spot where Lila had taken their picture yesterday. Closing his eyes, he did his best to reconstruct the scene, and after a bit he realized almost certainly that lousy Lila was right for once in her life, that the kid *didn't* have the doll with her on the steps, which meant she *did* leave it in the taxi, which meant Cuddly *would* be on Lambeth Street, just like Lila predicted. Contenting himself with the thought that at least he would be the one to bring it home, Amos got into the first cab that came along and said the lost and found, and on the way he wondered if Lila had had the sense to take her roll of pictures to be developed. Then he remembered she'd been using the Minox that he'd given her for the trip and it always took a while to develop them.

"Right here, guv," the driver said, not long later.

Amos paid him and then walked very quickly into the dank building and followed the sign to the second floor where the lost and found was. There were several windows, but only two were labeled 'Lost' and there were short lines for both. Amos chose the nearest, waiting patiently behind a cliché-type Britisher, dark suit, bowler and all. The two women behind the counters chatted away with each other while they did their work, and Amos thought that if they'd knock it off awhile, everything might move just a little bit faster. Still, things went surprisingly quickly and it wasn't long before the man in front of him was saying, "I left my umbrella by the Haymarket Theatre Saturday last. My wife inked my name on the thing. 'Hayworth.' Black umbrella. Quite large. Gnarly wood handle." "One moment, sir," the woman behind the counter said, and she disappeared into the back behind some frosted-glass room dividers.

Amos looked at the gentleman in front of him, openly admiring the way the man had stated his business. Wham-wham-wham—no wasted words, just the meat and that's it. No knuckling under in public. No squeamish stomachy flutters when a headwaiter heads your way. I wish I could do that, Amos thought, and then he thought, by Christ I can.

" 'Hayworth' did you say?" the women asked, returning to the window, empty-handed. "Nothing, sorry."

"Thank you," the man said, turning, going, gone.

Amos stepped up to the window. "My child lost her rag doll by St. Paul's yesterday morning. Nine inches long. No distinguishing features. But the hands are sewn together."

"Sorry, dearie," the woman said.

"What do you mean?"

"We haven't got it."

"But you didn't even go look?"

"I check everything before I come on."

"But he just asked you for an umbrella. If you checked everything, why'd you go check for him and not me?"

"All umbrellas look alike, dearie."

"So do rag dolls except this one had the hands—"

"We haven't got any rag dolls, dearie. We haven't had any rag dolls for weeks. We haven't had *any* dolls for weeks. Oh, one or two, but nothing like what you're looking for."

"I hate to be a nag, but—"

"Sorry, dearie, but—"

"—this is kind of a little bit important so—"

"Next, please?" the woman said.

From behind Amos, a feminine voice said, "I left my purse in the taxi on the way—"

Amos turned to the woman behind him. "Pardon me

one moment more, madam," he said, before turning back to the lady behind the counter. "You mean that's it?"

The woman sighed. "Dearie, I swear on bended knee I'm not cheating you out of your rag doll."

"I didn't mean to imply you were cheating."

"Of course you didn't. Bye, dearie."

Amos nodded and turned again, moving out of the room to the stairs and halfway down them before he sat. He put his elbows on his knees and his chin in his hands and tried to figure it all out. She should have looked. She shouldn't have just rebuffed him from memory. Looking was her job after all. Finding things that people asked her for. Not that it mattered; crucifyingly important it wasn't. Still, she should have at least had the decency to look.

Amos stood and made his way back up the stairs. She should have and he was going to ask her. Just point blank. 'I want you to take a look. For me. As a special favor. And thank you very much.'

But when he reached the room again his courage was quite gone so he got in the other 'lost' line instead. There was, after all, no point to a scene, and probably she was the type who would take it as a personal affront that her authority had been questioned and maybe she'd get stubborn so when all that could be avoided by just getting into the other line, why not avoid it? Amos nodded definitively, in total self-agreement, and waited in line. It was terribly hot again and he sweated as he stood there, and when his turn came, he said, very softly to the second lady so that the first lady wouldn't overhear, "I'd like a rag doll please."

"What's that, sir? You'll have to speak up." The second lady smiled.

"A rag doll," Amos repeated. "About so long," and held his hands approximately nine inches apart. "Hands all sewn together. I lost it yesterday at St. Paul's. My daughter did."

"Sorry, sir. Nothin' like that's been turned in."

"Could you look please?"

"There's no point in my looking, sir. I know the stock."

"It would really mean a lot to me if you'd just maybe take a look-see."

"We got any rag dolls back there?" the second lady said suddenly to the first.

"Please—" Amos began.

"Is it you again?" the first lady said.

Amos nodded. "It's me again."

"I'm telling you, dearie, there's nothing."

"I'm doing business with this lady now if you don't mind," Amos said. Then, softer, to the second lady: "I don't want to cause any trouble or anything but—"

"What do you mean you're doing business with her now?" the first lady said, coming over to the second lady's window. "I told you the truth before. If it'd been diamonds you lost, then maybe—"

"Listen," Amos put in. "Nobody's saying you didn't tell the truth. It just got to gnawing at me that maybe you were overlooking—"

"You people," the first lady said, and she walked back to the glass partition, glanced in, then came back to Amos. "Okay, I looked. There's nothing."

"You call that a look? My God there could be a zeppelin back there and you wouldn't have had time to see it."

"Who are you?" the second lady said.

"I'm just a lousy American tourist who's trying to find a rag doll so let's not make a thing about it."

"We're not the ones making a thing about it, dearie."

"I want to look at your stock," Amos said then.

"Not allowed."

"I'll keep my hands above my head every step of the way so you'll know I won't rob you blind."

"You're not allowed in the back, dearie. You're unauthorized personnel."

"I wanna look back there," Amos told her. "You're not, obviously, and one of us ought to, so I'm elected."

"What's the drama?" a man said, walking up to the women from behind the glass partitions.

"This fellow here—" the first lady began.

"Are you in charge?" Amos interrupted.

"I like to think so," the man said.

Amos took out his wallet. "See? Diner's Club, American Express. I'm not a crook. I just want to peek back there and see if maybe by some slip or something my kid's rag doll might be being overlooked. See, I know it is. We lost it in the taxi yesterday in front of St. Paul's and—"

"I'll go look again, for heaven's sakes," the first lady said.

"No!" from Amos.

The first lady turned on him. "Listen, dearie—do you want me to look or don't you?"

"You're mad," Amos said. "Sometimes people don't see so good when they're mad. Things get overlooked and—"

"You calling me a thief? You calling me a liar?"

"I'M NOT CALLING ANYBODY ANYTHING! I'M JUST GOING BACK THERE, THAT'S ALL! I DON'T CARE WHAT YOU DO AND I DON'T CARE WHAT YOU SAY, I'M GOING BACK THERE AND GET CUDDLY AND YOU'RE NOT GOING TO STOP ME!"

"He's crazy, Charley," the first lady whispered.

"He is." The second lady nodded. "Let him look. They go away after they look."

"Sure you can look, Mister," Charley said. "Look all you want to. Take your time," and he opened the connecting door for Amos and stood aside.

"I . . . " Amos said. "I'm not what you think . . . I'm not . . . " crazy, he was about to say. But then he thought: maybe I am.

So he just smiled instead.

"Wadja buy, wadja buy?" Lila called, the minute he started opening the door.

Amos made his way slowly into the room, holding out his empty hands. "Nothing. I just mostly window-shopped. Comparison pricing. Sportcoats and suits and like that."

"You look like death warmed over."

"My back's killing me." He took off his shoes and suit coat and lay down on the bed.

"What'd you do, hit every store in London?"

Amos shrugged. "Where's Jasmine?"

85

"In the other bathroom. Mrs. Piper's trying to get her clean but the odds are against it." Lila smiled and shook her head.

"You two had a good time, huh?"

"I guess."

"She really like Battersea Park, did she?"

"Ask her. She's nothing if not verbal."

Amos nodded and began jamming his knuckles into the base of his spine.

"Amos?"

"Hm?"

"Listen—I learned something. There's a lost and found office for all London taxis. On Lambeth Street. Any driver knows where it is."

"Very interesting," Amos said. "I'll have to remember that." He looked dead at his wife. "You two had a ball, huh? At Battersea Park I mean."

"I'm the leader," Jessica shouted then, running in. Mrs. Piper stayed in the doorway, more Mary-Poppins-like than Amos had even remembered.

"Are you the waiter with my gin and tonic?" Amos asked his child.

"You wanna see my balloons? I got so many balloons, all different colors."

"Your mother bought you balloons, eh? What else did you eat?"

"We didn't *eat* the balloons, we *carried* them."

"Oh."

"And you know what else?"

"What else?"

"Mommy found out where Cuddly is."

Amos sat up in bed.

"She's waiting for me on Lambeth Street. Mommy's gonna get her tomorrow."

"Baby—" Amos began.

"And Mommy bought me post cards too. Of all the places we been."

"Baby, Cuddly isn't there."

"How do *you* know?" Lila said.

"Come here, Josephine." He reached out for his daughter, took her hands. "Daddy spent the whole day looking for Cuddly. He tried just as hard as he could. He went to St. Paul's Cathedral and he went to Lambeth Street and Cuddly's just not there. I don't want you getting your hopes up when there's nothing to get them up about. She's lost. She's gone. But Daddy did all he could and the next doll you see you want Daddy will get you. Do you understand?"

"But Mommy said—"

"Listen to what Daddy says, never mind Mommy, okay?"

"Okay."

"Daddy loves you, baby. Daddy loves you more than anyone else in the world and he tried just as hard as he could to bring back Cuddly—he spent all afternoon trying to do it. But Cuddly's gone, baby, and even Daddy couldn't bring her back, do you understand? Daddy—"

"Why don't you run along now, Jessica," Lila said. "Go and show Mrs. Piper all the wonderful new toys and things you got today."

"All right, Mommy," Jessica said, and she ran from the room. Mrs. Piper followed her and Lila closed the connecting door softly, saying as she turned to her husband, "You lying son of a bitch."

"*What?*"

"Keep your voice down you lying bastard, she's right in the next room."

Amos got up off the bed.

"You like hell spent the day looking for Cuddly! You spent the day window-shopping for what you're gonna buy with the stinking money you made from that lousy crappy song except you're so sick you can't even spend a penny without first checking every store in town."

"You're very close to getting hit now, Lila, you ought to know that."

"You're a joke, Amos; that's what you are."

"*I* was supposed to take her to Battersea Park! That was *our* excursion. She wanted to go with me not with you and so while you were off doing what *I* was supposed to do I looked for that goddamned doll."

"You might as well keep on lying, you're in deep enough—"

"I know what you're trying to do—trying to worm your way in with the kid—gonna take her to see the Mets when we get back? You're a crappy mother and nothing's gonna change that so—"

"*Let's—just—get—it—done.*"

"Get what done?"

"*Divorced!*"

"What are you talking about?" Amos said. He sat back down on the bed.

"Oh Amos stop lying. This whole assy trip was supposed to save our marriage. I know it and you know it so—"

"—I've never in my life even thought of leaving you—"

"—Amos—*stop*—"

"—and I *did* spend the day looking for Cuddly—"

"—*stop* I said—"

"—I'll describe the Lambeth Street place to you—"

"—How would I know I've never been there—"

"—it's on the second floor—"

"—*I've never been there, Amos*—"

"—well I have because I care for the kid—"

"—and I don't?—"

"—you said it—"

"—God you're so crazy—"

"—the kid wants me—"

"—she wants me—"

"—like hell—"

"—I'll get her, ask any judge—"

"—never—"

"—what about a divorce?—"

'Swell!' he almost said. 'Great! Yes!' as he rose in wrath from the bed, advancing dead at her, his right hand raised to strike her down, until across what was left of his brain the steaming message flashed that he needed them, both, his child *and* his wife, only his wife didn't need him, not any more, not from her face. So more in anguish even than surprise, he dropped his hand and veered from the suicide course, saying, "Let's get out of here, Lila. Just you and me. Let's take off! Let's fly!"

"The Jews have spoiled it," Lila was saying.

Amos glanced quickly up from the overstuffed chair. "Spoiled what?"

Lila gestured toward the window. "Rome."

Amos stood and moved to the window, staring out at the stunning view of the Spanish Steps and beyond it, the Via Condotti which, even though it resembled Greenwich Village, was probably as fine a street for shopping as any in the world. They had just finished unpacking and the air conditioner was going full blast and as he looked around, Amos wondered if a better hotel than the Hassler was possible. "Who told you that?"

"Mother."

"Then we quick better engrave the words in stone."

"Mother says Rome used to be the place until after the war. Then the Jews came. You know how she claims they all made their fortunes in the blackmarket. Now she says you can't take a step without them swarming all over you." Lila began imitating her mother. "They just swarm all over you, Lila. It's terrible. Paris is nothing any more. Now they've ruined Rome. I tell you, no place is safe from them, close quote."

"The soul of a saint, the heart of a poet, that's your mommy."

"You're very quick to knock her when she's not around, you ever notice that?"

"I'd do it to her face," Amos said, "except I'm a coward. And she's stronger than I am."

"Strong she is," Lila said. "All a hundred and five pounds of her."

The telephone rang.

"Bombs away," Amos said.

Lila nodded and picked up the receiver. "Thank you," she said. "Yes, I'll wait."

"Her?" Amos asked.

Lila nodded again then burst into *"Moth*er, hiiiiiii."

"Let's take it again from the top and show a little enthusiasm," Amos said.

Lila waved him silent. "Yes, we're really in Rome. Just got here." She paused. "Jessica's back in London and she's fine. We left her with Mary Poppins so I don't think too much can go wrong. How are you, Mother?" There was a considerable pause. "Well isn't that the limit?" Lila said then. "Let me tell Amos, he's right here. Amos, there's a water shortage in New York again."

"Lucky for your mother she only drinks blood."

Lila slapped her hand over the receiver. "Will you just watch it—let me know when you're gonna come out with those."

Amos beamed.

"He thinks it's just an outrage, Mother."

Amos walked to the window and stared out.

"We're fine, Mother. I'm only calling because I didn't want you trying to get us in London and having a snit when we weren't there."

There was a pause.

"No I mean it, Mother—the trip's even better than we hoped. We just thought as long as we were so close to Italy and Amos had always wanted to see it we were fools not to come. So we're here for a day or three and then off to Venice and then London again."

Pause.

"We didn't bring Jessica because we thought it would be too much for her."

Pause.

"Of course I'm telling you the truth. I tell you Amos is positively manic and I'm as chipper as can be."

"Ask her if she'd like me to ship her a little plasma," Amos said from the window.

"That was just Amos cracking wise, Mother. I just told you he was manic these days."

"Ask her if she's heard the Jews have ruined Rome?"

"You're right, Mother; he is a scream."

Pause.

"You're getting to be a bore on the subject, Mother. We left her behind because we left her behind and we came to Italy because we came to Italy."

Pause.

"We wanted a couple of days to ourselves, Mother; what's wrong with that?"

Long pause.

"Mother—Mother listen—Mother, *you* left *me* all the time, Mother—you were forever leaving me with some servant or other. You're getting senile if you think you never left me."

Pause.

"Mother, there's not a damn thing wrong with parents leaving their kid with Mary Poppins. Now I'll call you again from London. After Venice. Now that'll just be a couple of days so don't worry. Goodbye, Mother, yes, of course I know you love me. Goodbye." She held the receiver a moment, then dropped it into its cradle.

"She knows we got troubles, huh?" Amos asked.

Lila nodded.

"She's probably calling up Madame Nhu right now to give the good news."

Lila stood mute above the phone.

Amos went to her. "Snap to, baby—it's one in the afternoon and your mother can't leave her grave till nightfall. Now c'mon: let's go get Nino," Nino being Amos' discovery at the airport, less than two hours before.

He and Lila had taken different planes from London, which was probably silly but Amos would never fly with his wife unless the kid was along too. Their planes were supposed to arrive at the same time but Amos got in first and, after zipping through customs, he lugged his bag around da Vinci airport, phrase book in hand, saying to anyone who looked remotely like a taxi driver, *"Parla inglese?"* but no one did, and Amos' back was beginning to give with the weight of his suitcase when from behind him came the words, "I speak."

Amos turned, trying not to gape at the size of the man before him. At least six-four, Amos decided, with arms like legs and black curly hair covering a face surprisingly sweet, except for an enormous jagged scar along the left cheek and temple. "You do?"

"I speak terrific," the giant said.

"Hassler?" Amos said.

"Terrific," again, and he reached down for Amos' bag.

Amos flipped frantically through his phrase book for the word 'stop,' finally, with relief, muttering *"Macchia. Macchia."*

A confused look covered the enormous head. *"Macchia?"*

"Si," Amos said, and then he started laughing because in his hurry he had given the word for 'spot' instead. *"Scusi,"* Amos said. "I meant *'alt.'* "

The giant put the bag down.

"You'll have to bear with me it's complicated," Amos began, flipping through his phrase book again. "See, *mio moglie* is coming on another *aereo,* and she's due in any *secondo* so we'll just *aspettare* until she gets here. *Capisco?*"

"You have children, yes? That is why you fly apart."

"Hey you really do speak."

The giant head nodded.

"Terrific," Amos said.

Lila arrived a few minutes later and Amos embraced her briefly before indicating Nino who stood waiting at a distance. "He's just a pup," Amos said and Lila said, "Let's hope he's friendly," and then Nino was leading them out of the airport into the Italian heat. He carried all their luggage under one arm and with the other arm he pointed. "Mine," he said.

Amos approached the Mercedes. "You own this?"

"Each year more," came the reply. "How you call it?—"

"Installment plan?" Lila volunteered.

"Installment plan, yes. I pay a little every month. It will be all mine when I am only a hundred and forty-six years old. Please now," and he proudly held open the door. "Enter."

They got in and made themselves comfortable while he set their luggage in the trunk. Then he got in the front, started the smooth motor. "Rome is not for twenty-five miles yet," he said then. "I will tell you when to start looking."

"How was your flight?" Amos asked, as the car left the airport.

"Flying doesn't bother me, you know that. I don't guess I cried for more than an hour."

Amos smiled and contemplated taking his wife's hand. She was wearing white, and her hair had recovered from Vidal Sassoon, and she looked, in all ways, splendid. "Great dress," Amos said. "New?"

"Nice try, Amos, but I wore it the night we got engaged."

Goddamit I knew it looked familiar, Amos thought, saying "You've got to know I was kidding" while he thought it.

"Considering our conditions, I believe you."

Then the driver began to sing 'Francie' out loud.

"I'm sorry I said it was a crappy song," Lila began. "I think it's a fine song."

"Considering our conditions, I believe you," Amos answered, leaning forward, tapping the giant's shoulder. "You like that song?"

"The Francie song you mean?"

"You like it a lot, do you?"

"Terrific."

"You think it's good, yes?"

"*Molto bene.* You understand *molto bene?*"

Amos nodded. "I wrote it."

The car pulled without warning off the highway and stopped. "You wrote it?"

"*Si.*"

"You wrote that song?"

"*Si.*"

"The music, yes?"

"Yes."

"Not the words too."

"The words too."

"Both you wrote?"

"Yes."

"Sign please, your name?" and he produced a printed card and a yellow stub of a pencil. "You are the most famous man I have ever drove."

Amos flushed and signed his name, noting the giant's was Nino Something-long-and-terribly-Italian.

"*Grazie, grazie,*" Nino said, and he produced a chauffeur's cap from the seat beside him. "For you," he said to Amos, as he put it on. Then he set the car in motion again, pulling smoothly back onto the highway.

"I never remember you doing that before," Lila said as Amos sat back, clearly triumphant.

"Do what?"

"Tell anybody anything. Volunteer it like that."

Amos shrugged. "My wife's about to leave me: I'll try anything."

Lila nodded.

"Nino?" Amos said then.

"Yes Mister Composer?"

"Your card, it said you were a guide."

"In all Rome there is none more terrific guide than me. I said that right?"

"*Molto bene,*" Amos said. "You want to guide us to St. Peter's after we check in?"

"Sunday is not so terrific for going to St. Peter's."

"Where should we go?"

"I will please you."

"Okay. We'll just check in, then take off."

"After I call Mother," Lila said.

And after she did they saw Rome. First they went to the of course Colosseum, which Amos was against when Nino said it, because it was so corny, the Colosseum, on all the post cards anyway, but when they got close and Amos saw the darn thing, actually saw it, it killed him, just like the Largo Argentina killed Lila, what with all the dozens of cats rollicking around the ruins. And they zipped through the Borghese Gardens and along the Via Veneto which Amos had been dying to see ever since Fellini except that when you got there what you saw was two, maybe three blocks of sidewalk cafés with everybody from Dubuque looking at everyone else from Dubuque and wondering where the hell was Sophia Loren. And they went to the Piazza Venezia where Nino pointed out the balcony Mussolini used to harangue the crowds, and after that, because it was so hot, they stopped for some of the ice cream at Tre Scalini which, Amos decided after his first orgiastic nibble, was to American ice cream as Willie Mays was to Ron Swaboda.

Then they got going again, roaring through the silent city without ever worrying about traffic since, Nino informed them, everyone with a car was at the beach. They saw more piazzas and ruins than Amos knew existed, and as the afternoon came to a close, he decided that what he really wanted was for some producer to translate *Francie* into Italian and put it on in Rome, with the sole stipulation that the composer, one Amos McCracken, come along with his family as artistic adviser and live in town awhile.

They returned to the Hassler after seven, beat, making arrangements for Nino to meet them the next morning at ten, please, and Amos asked if he wanted to get paid now for this day's labor. Nino hesitated a moment before answering. Awaiting the reply, Amos thought that a strange look crossed the giant's scarred face. Then the answer: "I'm not worried about getting my money, Mister Composer."

Amos and Lila showered and changed and dined on the Hassler Roof. As they watched the sun die over the Spanish Steps, Amos realized what a wise man he had been, coming to Rome. Because twice during dinner Lila smiled at him, and once he made her laugh, and partially that was because he was not without humor, but partially too, it was the place. You laughed a lot in Rome. You laughed a lot and you screwed a lot and you patched things up when they were torn. That was what Rome was there for. To heal you.

Later, in bed in darkness, Amos was all set for a little action. When he heard Lila's breathing deepen into sleep, he knew she was kidding, until he reached out and touched her. Then he lay back. He was ordinarily a poor sleeper, but since the London explosion, he had become impossible. He had never known, in his bachelor days, how he had won Lila. He had less idea, now, how he was losing her. "You might've at least said good night," Amos muttered.

Then he reached for his kneecaps and started playing tunes.

The next morning at ten, Nino was waiting by his Mercedes. "Where to?" Amos asked, as they got in.

"I would like to suggest," Nino said. "A surprise. A place you never heard. Maybe you will think it is terrific. My surprise for you and your song. I can take you there?"

"What is it?" Amos asked.

Lila shook her head. "You're just like Jessica blabbing secrets. How can it be a surprise if he tells us? Nino, lead on."

"Right, right, right," Amos said, sitting back in the car. "Nino, we're in your hands," and he smiled, broadly, because he hated surprises, they frightened him, always, always.

Nino began to drive.

"Hey, this is really a treat, y'know, Lila?"

Lila gave him a look.

"What're you looking at me like that for?" Amos asked.

Very softly Lila said, "When you say something in that tone of voice, I don't know what it means except it doesn't mean what you're saying."

"You trying to irritate me? You know how it irritates me when you mind-read like that."

Lila dropped her voice still further. "Don't ruin this."

"What?" Amos whispered back.

"He's so excited. Just don't ruin it, huh Amos?"

"Oh for chrissakes," Amos said and he stared out the window as the Mercedes raced through Rome. He stayed quiet for as long as he could. Then he said, "Nino?"

"Yes, Mister Composer?"

"We almost there yet?"

"It is out of town," Nino answered. "I didn't tell you?"

"No," Amos said. "But it doesn't matter." He smiled again, cursing himself for his nut paranoia, because all he could think was that he was driving out of a strange city with a giant whose last name he didn't know, to a place he didn't know, and not only that, but no one knew he was going, so if anything happened, no one would know he was gone, and in his passport wallet, bulging now from his inside coat pocket, was over two thousand dollars in cash and traveler's checks and you could pay a lot of Mercedes installments with two thousand dollars and then he remembered the strange look that had come across Nino's face the night before and his words, 'I'm not worried about getting my money, Mister Composer,' and for the first time, as the car left the city behind, Amos found himself genuinely curious as to just how Nino got the enormous scar that ran so cruelly from his cheek, up past his ear, to his temple.

They stayed on the main road for several miles and then turned right, onto a smaller road, narrow and dusty but more often than not paved, and they stayed on that road until they reached a small, unattractive village.

"Gee, what a picturesque place," Amos said. "Wouldn't you like some pictures of that, Lila?"

"Not particularly," Lila said.

Amos was about to demand that the car stop but suddenly they took a very sharp left, moving onto a still narrower road, and the ugly village was behind them. "That place," Nino said, not turning around but gesturing back in the direction of the ugly village. "A hicktown." He turned then, smiling, but Amos saw only the scar. "I just remember that word. Hicktown. Mrs. Composer? The truth?"

"Anything, Nino."

"My speaking, it is already more terrific today than yesterday, yes?"

Lila nodded. "It really is. You speak wonderfully, Nino."

"That is because I learn in America."

"When were you in America?" Lila asked.

"Nineteen and forty-two till forty-six." He turned again with another smile. "I was prisoner of war."

As soon as Nino turned back to the road, Amos tried getting Lila's attention without Nino's noticing in the rearview mirror, but she ignored him, leaning forward, her head on the back of the front seat, talking to him. "Really?" she said. "Tell me about it."

Nino fingered his scar. "This you have seen."

"Whatzat?" Amos said quickly. "Oh. Funny how you never notice things till they're pointed out to you."

"It was not so terrific when it happen. Africa. Then a lot of hospital. Then America. Texas, first. Texas is not so terrific either. But after Texas, San Francisco. Two years, almost three. A mechanic. I work on trucks and cars. That is where I learn to speak."

"Everybody treat you nice?" Amos asked. "In America?"

"Some did. But you know, there was the war on."

They were climbing precariously up the remnants of the road now, alone and unseen. He hates Americans, Amos realized. We shoved his face in it for four years and now—

"Mister Composer?"

"What is it what?" Amos said, obviously in a strange way, for Lila looked at him. He tried explaining with his eyes but she missed it, missed it all, which was typical. Back when they started out, she was mind-reading him, now, when he needed her, she was giving him looks, then turning and staring out the window.

The earth continued to fall away beneath them. "From a song like your song, can you stop work forever if you want?"

"You mean, do I make a lot of money? Actually, Nino, I don't really make much at all. To begin with, you see, my publisher takes—" But he stopped then, because

Lila was watching him again and he didn't like her eyes.

"I have always dream of that. Of making so much *denaro* all at one time I could stop everything."

Lila said, "What would you do if you could retire, Nino?"

Amos snapped his fingers. "Lila—Lila listen a sec—do you know what I did? I left all our money back at the hotel, is that stupid?"

"What're you talking about?" Lila said.

"Our money. I'm telling you about how I left all our money in the room, how do you like that?"

"Amos it's in your wallet."

"Right. And I left my wallet—"

"Amos I can see it bulging." She reached toward his coat pocket.

Amos grabbed her hand. "The *other* wallet, Lila. The wallet I keep my money in. That's—"

"You don't have any other—"

"*We got no money, Lila.* Not with us. That's the thing to remember. Not a lira or a sou. So if anything happened to us, we couldn't pay—"

"Omigod," Lila said, and she sat back, away from Amos, ripping her hand from his. And then, in a whisper: "It's hopeless with you, Amos. It just is."

"If I could retire?" Nino said, pointing high ahead of them. "I would come home."

Amos looked up ahead and there, rising sheer from the valley floor was the tallest hill he had ever seen, a great rocky thing, beaten desperately by the weather but not to death, and perched on top, somehow also precariously alive, was a tiny village, the houses also rock, the

103

same color as the hill, so that except for the few tiny windows, it was impossible to tell where the one ended, where the other began, and Amos thought, in its own way, it competed with St. Paul's.

"That's your home? Up there?" he asked.

Nino nodded. "Until the war. Also it is my surprise. For you, Mister Composer. For your song. Maybe you think it is terrific?"

"It is, it really is," and he reached out, patting the giant gently on the shoulder. The car ascended toward the tiny village and Amos thought that she was right, Lila. He was hopeless. Crazy and hopeless and everything he touched turned to shit.

"From here we have to walk," Nino said at the start of the village. "Take your time. Look. See? We have the radio here. I will tell them who you are—they know your song. But I will tell them not to bother you." He led the way into the village, Amos behind him, Lila, silent, last.

"How old is this?" Amos asked.

"Five hundred years? Six hundred?" Nino shrugged. "Old." He gave a little bow, *"Scusi,"* and walked away.

"Listen, I'm sorry," Amos said, when Nino was gone.

"I know. You can't help it."

"Let's not make out like I'm raving, Lila. I got this buggy idea, I'll admit, but it wasn't malicious or anything, give me that."

"Okay."

They walked over the old stones beneath the aged arches. From various windows and doorways, black-shawled women eyed them and slender children darted out from corners, then skittered away. Amos and Lila walked in silence for no more than a moment and found themselves suddenly at the end of the village. A low walled fence and then nothing; a drop sheer and clean to the valley below. The air was very cool, and the constant wind stroked their faces. It was one of those sights you remember, and Amos, as he reached blindly for his wife, knew as he was reaching that she would pull away, but into his arms she came and it wasn't till he kissed her that he realized how much better it would have been if she *had* pulled away, because she responded like rock until he released her, and then she started talking, soft and sad: "Oh, Amos, there's this terrible thing going on. You're just not charming any more and what am I going to do? I knew you were a nut when I married you, but you were so charming then and I loved it, the unpredicatability, but I can't cope with you now. I'm tired of the fighting and I'm tired of the joking and I'm tired of being the villain of the piece. I asked you not to ruin this today. Here was this dear sweet man with this poor scarred face and he wanted to show us something so much he was just like a baby. And you had to go ahead and ruin it. I'm twenty-seven years old and I'm ready for menopause. You've run me out of resources. I'm dry." She left him then, slowly, making her way back to the car.

Amos looked out at the valley, then up to the houses rising from the rock, thinking, if you can endure, we can endure. If you can face the wind, we can face each other. Me and Lila. Lila and me.

But dear God, I gotta do something soon.

It was almost the end of siesta when they finished sight-seeing and returned to the Hassler. They napped, longer than they'd planned, and before they began dressing hurriedly for a shopping trip, six o'clock had come and gone. All the stores stayed open till eight, having closed from one to four, and Amos, ready first, excused himself and zipped downstairs to the main lobby where he sought out the hall porter or concierge or whatever you called such wizards in Italy, and he asked the concierge the key question, got the answer, and when he returned to Lila he was *up*.

"What are you so giddy about?" Lila wondered, applying a final coat of lipstick with ultimate concentration.

"Anytime I don't hafta wait a year and a half for you to be ready, it affects me this way," Amos answered.

"Unfair," Lila said. "I'm not that bad any more. I'm a lot faster than I used to be."

Amos held the door open for her. "Have you ever thought of what would have happened if you were any *slower* than you used to be? By the time you'd be ready to face the day, it'd be smack in the middle of the after-theatre rush."

They waited for the elevator, taking it down to the lobby. The concierge nodded at Amos, and Amos, when Lila was looking the other way, made a circle with his thumb and index finger and winked. Away from the hotel they paused a moment. It wasn't cool, but the vicious heat of the day had been dissipated. Amos took his wife's hand as they descended the Spanish Steps toward the Via Condotti, released it finally when they got there.

"Do we want to buy anything for anyone back home?"

Lila asked. "Anything special I mean. Were we given requests?"

"Donny Klein asked could we send him Claudia Cardinale but I think you have to get her on the next street over." He moved nervously several paces ahead.

"Let's just take it easy then and window-shop."

"I hate window-shopping, you know that."

Lila actually threw up her hands. "Amos, the whole purpose of this was to window-shop. You said so. Why do you act this way?"

A little faith, Amos thought, and I'll make you smile.

"You just can't tell when I'm kidding any more, Lila. Senility has that effect on some, I'm told." He stopped in front of a leather shop. "Hey, here's a terrific leather beach bag Gucci's giving away practically for only a trillion lira. Would you like it? Don't let the price tag upset you; that's only a billion Yankee dollars."

Lila stared in the Gucci window. "What a gorgeous store. You know, leather's supposed to be a good buy in Italy. Do we need anything in leather?"

"I'm a little low on leather underwear."

"You're really manic tonight," Lila said, ambling to the next store, a boutique.

Hurry it up please. It's almost seven. I beg you. Just this one time let's do something right.

"You know what I'd like?" Lila said. "Some plain flat leather sandals."

"Listen, we'll have 'em for supper, how's that, now come on."

"Where are we going?"

"Nowhere special but these boutiques aren't for me—

I can't wear their clothes. I mean, you gotta consider my feelings, Lila. What time is it?"

Lila looked at her hated Timex. "Seven nearly."

"Hey, there's supposed to be this terrific clothing place up ahead a ways, so would you just hop to it till we get there? Please?"

"It's like shopping with Jessica—next thing you'll be asking for a piece of penny gum," but she started walking faster.

Amos pointed along the crowded narrow street. "It's along here somewheres."

"Then after that we'll look for some sandals for me, deal?"

"Deal."

They hurried along the Via Condotti, Amos leading the way, threading a path for Lila to follow. Whenever he got too far ahead he always stopped until she had him in sight again before hurrying on.

Then he was there. "Lila," he called. "C'mere a sec."

She caught up to him.

Amos pointed through the showcase window. "You see that alarm clock? The one in red leather."

"So?"

"I just wonder how much it is."

"I thought you were looking for a clothing store."

"Come on in with me. It won't take a minute." He held the door open for her and they entered the quiet elegant store. In the rear, a carpeted staircase led to a balcony, and all around the store, beautifully displayed, was every kind of timepiece from chronometers to sundials. A young plump saleslady approached them.

"*Scusi*," Amos began. "*Parla inglese?*"

With almost no trace of accent, the saleslady said, "Yes sir, I do."

"Well," Amos told her, indicating on a note of triumph his blond wife in the doorway, "this lady here is looking for a gold watch with a gold band."

Lila just stood there.

"Surprise, surprise," Amos said. "You've only wanted one for about a thousand years."

"Amos—" Lila began.

"Would the lady care for a seat?" the salesgirl said, indicating a chair by a glass counter.

"The lady could use one I think," Amos said, and he escorted Lila to the chair and sat her down.

"You sneak," Lila said.

Amos bowed.

Lila beckoned for him to bend close. "This place looks awfully expensive," she whispered.

"Actually it's very cheap," Amos whispered back. "All their merchandise is stolen."

"What kind of watch did you have in mind?" the salesgirl asked. She was about the same age as Lila, but perhaps twice as heavy, and as dark as Lila was fair. Her left eye blinked constantly, an unkind tic, lending her face the effect of continual flirtation.

Lila gestured helplessly. "I didn't really have a watch in mind. I don't know."

"A gold watch with a gold band," Amos said. "Within that framework."

"Have you any preference? Would you like a large watch? Small? Very thin?"

Lila just shook her head.

The salesgirl smiled. "Perhaps I should just show you," and she walked a few paces away, bending down behind the glass counter.

"I don't need any gold watch," Lila whispered. "What have I done to deserve a gold watch?"

"Shut up," Amos said.

"Amos I just don't deserve one."

"Lila—"

"My Timex never loses a minute—"

"Lila, how many times have you wished for a gold watch? In my presence. How many jewelry shop windows have we gaped through?"

"That was all just pretend stuff. I was never seriously contemplating—I mean, they're so expensive—"

"They're very good buys here, does that make you feel better?"

"Why don't we start with these," the salesgirl said, her left eye flirting with Amos. She set down a dark, felt tray with more than a dozen watches on it.

"Oh isn't that beautiful," Lila said. "I want them all."

The salesgirl smiled. "We do have a very nice selection."

"I don't want to sound like a tourist," Lila said, "but would these cost as much in America do you think?"

"Perhaps two times more."

"Then it really isn't, I mean, I wouldn't be being a spendthrift for buying one."

The salesgirl smiled a pudgy smile and shook her head, while her left eye continued its flirtation.

Lila stared at the tray of gold watches. "Where should I begin?"

The salesgirl lifted up a lovely gold watch. "This is pretty, I think."

Lila held out her arm, then pulled it back, jerked off her Timex and stuffed it in her purse. Then she held up her arm again. The salesgirl put the gold watch around her wrist. "What do you think?" Lila asked Amos, who had pulled up another chair and was sitting down.

"My stock answer will be 'beautiful.' It's up to you, baby."

"But you've got to look at it."

"And *you've* got to wear it so knock it off please."

Lila smiled at the salesgirl. "I really don't deserve one," she said. She examined the watch on her wrist. "It's beautiful," she said. "I'll—" she looked at Amos. "I was going to say 'I'll take it' but that's silly isn't it, grabbing at the first thing you see. As long as I'm buying a watch, I ought to think a little, right?"

"Right," Amos said.

The salesgirl took the first watch off Lila's wrist, put another on. "Slightly more formal," she said. "But yet still quite plain."

"It's beautiful too," Lila said.

Amos nodded.

"Maybe I should get this one."

Amos shrugged.

"Some help you are," Lila said. "Could I have a peek at that one there please?" and she indicated a third watch in the center of the tray.

The saleslady nodded. "Very thin, perfectly plain yet elegant, excellent for day or evening wear." She put it on Lila's wrist.

"Now that may be just what I'm looking for. Amos?"

"I refuse to answer on the grounds that it might tend to incriminate me."

"You don't like it, then."

"You don't suck me in that way, baby. You pick it out and I'll buy it. With my money and your taste the world is ours."

Lila exhaled and shook her head. "Is this your complete selection?"

The saleslady shook her head. "Just one moment," and she excused herself, returning a moment later with another tray of gold watches. Her left eye was beating faster now.

"*Ah*, now these look like the thing," Lila said.

Amos stared at the thirty-some-odd watches spread before them, and didn't notice the tall uniformed man who moved into the corner behind the saleslady until Lila whispered, "I feel like we're in a spy novel now."

"How come?" Amos whispered back.

Lila nodded faintly in the direction of the uniformed man. "He's here to guard the merchandise," she whispered.

Amos glanced casually up at the man. "Who the hell they think I am, Jimmy Valentine?"

"They always do it in stores like this." Then she turned to the saleslady. "You close at eight so I've got to make my mind up by then."

The saleslady smiled.

By the time the third tray of watches had been brought out, making a total of close to fifty, Amos stood up and stretched. He had only been seeing Dr. Marx for six months but it was long enough for him to recognize a psychological block when one hit him in the face, and Lila, glutted with gold watches, was going through something like that now. He sauntered casually away from his wife and began examining the store. It was very lovely, everything elegantly displayed, and a grandfather clock in the far corner caught his attention. Amos was more than ignorant of antiques but some things you could still spot no matter how ignorant you were, and this clock was beautiful, with clean sharp lines, a pendulum that fairly sparkled as it swung. Amos examined the clock for as long as he could, then returned to the trays. "How we coming?"

"Well not so good," Lila answered. "It isn't easy, buying a watch."

"You're wrong and I'll prove it," he told her before turning to the saleslady. "You got anything with one of those timer dinguses?"

She stooped, brought out a watch saying, "This is made especially for us in Switz—"

"I'll take it," Amos said. "What do I owe you?"

"That will be seventy-five dollars." The left eye picked up speed.

"See how simple?" Amos said to Lila as he filled out the proper amount of traveler's checks. He took his own watch off and put the new one on, pleased because he had always wanted a stop watch and because the first one she showed him was exactly what he had been looking for.

"Your change, sir," the saleslady said, when she came back.

Through it all, the guard in the corner never moved.

"How much are these gold ones though?" Lila asked then.

The saleslady began moving her hand quickly across the trays. "Two hundred, three hundred, three hundred, four hundred, three hundred—"

"Wow," Lila said. "And in the States they'd be almost twice as much?"

"I think so."

"What if I dropped it, Amos? That's eight hundred dollars down the drain."

"Perhaps if I took some of the trays away, your decision might be simpler."

"Please leave them out," Lila said. "It somehow makes it easier when I can see them all."

"As you wish," the salesgirl said, left eye moving.

"Maybe I can help," Amos said. "Just answer me a few simple questions. Do you want it round or oblong or rectangular or what?"

"I don't think oblong."

"How about fat or thin?"

"Thin."

"And the band, wide or narrow?"

"That depends on the watch, Amos. You wouldn't put a wide band with a teeny watch or a narrow band on a great clunk of a thing."

"You said you don't want a great clunk of a thing."

"No, I said I didn't want it fat. There's a difference."

"Lila—" Amos began, about to say 'for chrissakes

make up your cotton-picking mind,' but he stopped himself blessedly in time because he cared for her and needed her and when she had that gold watch on her wrist she'd know she needed him too. Don't blow it, Amos told himself. Maintain, at any cost, your cool. "You are a great nut," Amos said and he bent forward, kissing his wife quickly on the forehead, before retreating again to the far corner and the beauties of the old grandfather clock. His beautiful-new-bought-with-no-sweat-stop-watch said fifteen and a half minutes before eight o'clock which meant that somehow they had spent close to three quarters of an hour on what should have taken no more than two shakes at best, but then women were thank God women and dizzy about some things, like purchasing, so there was nothing for him to do but smile and wait. *Goddamit I wish to hell she'd hurry,* Amos thought, drumming his fingers against the side of the grandfather clock.

It was almost eight when Lila put her arm in his saying, "Shall we?"

"Which one'd you pick?"

"I'm coming back tomorrow bright and early for the final choice."

"You mean you didn't get one?"

"Now Amos—"

"Lila—" He looked over toward the pudgy salesgirl who stood behind the counter, the three large trays of gold watches still before her. "Sorry," Amos said, somehow managing control. *"Buona sera,"* and he headed for the door that led out to the Via Condotti, but the guard blocked their way.

"Scusi," the guard said.

Amos looked up at the gaunt uniformed man. "We're done," he explained. "We're just leaving."

"Manca un orologio d'oro. Forse sta nella borsa della signora."

The salesgirl came running over, left eye out of control.

"What'd he say?" Amos asked her.

The salesgirl smiled. "He says that somehow, by accident, perhaps one of our gold watches found its way into your wife's purse by mistake."

"Manco un orologio d'oro," the guard said again. *"Li ho contati me stresso."*

"He says he counted the watches and there is one missing."

"Li ho contati due volte. Non puo essere uno sbaglio."

"Two times he counted," the salesgirl explained. "He is very positive about it."

Amos glared up at the gaunt man. "Just because there's a watch missing doesn't mean it *has* to be in my wife's purse, y'know."

Lila started to open her purse.

"Shut that!" Amos told her.

Lila looked at him. "Why should I shut it?"

"Because I said so," Amos answered.

"Non l'ho vista metterlo nella borsa, ma non c'e altro posto dove potrebb'erre."

"He says he didn't actually see the accident—when she misplaced the watch into her purse—but he is positive it is there. He has been with us many years. He is very accurate." She covered her left eye with her hand and tried to smile.

"Well why don't I just open my purse and settle this thing," Lila said, and she started to open it again.

Amos grabbed it from her hands. "They're as much as calling you a thief, Lila." He turned to the saleslady. "Ask him if he's calling us thieves?"

"*Il signore vuole sapere se Lei lo chiami un ladro?*"

"*Manca un orologio. I nomi non c'entrano afatto.*"

"He says there is a watch missing and—"

"*Si, io credo che Lei abia preso l'orologio. Non c'e alto posto dove puo essere.*"

"There is no other place for the watch than your wife's purse, he says."

"In other words," Amos said, "he is calling us thieves."

"Truly," the salesgirl said. "Everyone makes mistakes. Now if you would just return the watch—"

Amos shook his head. "Just because *you* people misplace a watch doesn't mean that *we* are The Purple Gang. I'd like an apology from somebody, if you don't mind."

"Amos for God's sake, let's just open my purse and get the hell out of here."

Amos whirled on her. "It's like a loyalty oath, honey, don't you get that? Some things you just don't do. You don't sign loyalty oaths and you don't open purses when some bimbo claims you're a crook. It's principle, dammit, don't you see? Principle!"

"Why does *your* lousy principle always cause *us* trouble, tell me that?"

"I'd like to thank all my fans for their loyal support,"

117

Amos said. He turned back to the salesgirl. "We are not thieves," he said. "We are just plain crummy American tourists who love your city very much and don't want any trouble. Now if you would pleased extend to us the courtesy of an apology, we will be on our way."

"There is a watch missing," the girl said, left eye beating terribly.

"That's not our fault," Amos said.

"Perhaps I'd better get the manager," the girl said, and she disappeared up the stairs at the rear of the store hurrying toward the balcony.

"And it's another rip-roaring day in the life of Amos and Andy," Lila said, shaking her head, slowly crossing back to where the chairs were set up by the counters. Amos walked with her, half a step behind.

"*No-no-no-no-no!*" the guard shouted, running around them, heading them off, standing firmly between them and the watches that still covered the counter.

"Jesus," Amos said. "He thinks we're gonna pocket some more."

Lila looked around for another chair, saw none, so she flopped to the floor like a weary child, sitting cross-legged, her chin in her hands.

"What're you doing down there, Lila?"

"I felt like it."

Amos sat delicately down on the floor beside her, careful not to put strain on his back. "I think we give a very adult impression, don't you?"

Lila said nothing.

"And do me one favor. In the future, quit saying you'll open your purse every time you get a chance."

118

"I know you'd never let me, and besides, one of us just had to look honest."

"Explain both those statements if you don't mind."

Lila sighed. "Amos, if I knew one thing in this world I knew you'd rather go to the cross than let me open my purse. You and your 'principle' are not totally unfamiliar to me. I also knew they thought we were crooks."

"Why, for God's sake?"

"Oh use your head. We come in like gangbusters and get gold watches spread over the place and I ask her not to put them back and you come in and buy something less expensive out of the blue and pay for it which is only supposed to put them off their guard so they won't pay attention when I shovel the booty into my purse and we take off. Not only are we thieves, I think we're kinda skilled." She shook her head then. "I knew something was gonna happen. Something always happens whenever I buy a gold watch."

"You do it every day, do you?"

Lila shook her head. "Two times. Two times in all my life. The other was with Daddy. Mother had just eaten him alive and left him for dead. They'd only been divorced a little and he somehow got the loot together to come east for my birthday. I wasn't very old. Not even ten. I loved him so, Amos. God was he a failure. No drive and not enough talent—just funny and sweet and kind of dumb about people, especially Mother. She didn't want him seeing me on my birthday and there was this big stink about it I remember, but finally she gave him a couple of hours the day before and he said once we were alone, what did I want for a present and I said a

gold watch and he said 'then that's what you'll have' and
off we taxied. We went to one of those Fifth Avenue
places, I don't remember, and the salesman was very formal and Daddy said, God—it's crazy the way you remember things—he said, 'the best in the house for my
baby.' And the salesman bowed and scraped and I gig-
gled and wanted to bawl I guess I was so happy and then
the salesman slipped this teeny weeny gold watch on my
wrist and I loved it, naturally, and Daddy said 'it's
yours' so everything was perfect except he didn't have
enough money to pay for it. The bastard of a salesman
had put a real goddam gold watch on me and Daddy had
to crawl and try to joke his way out of it all the time
promising me he'd get it for me tomorrow but all I could
think was how much I wanted to die because my daddy
had to crawl and beg because I was such a stupid spoiled
bitch to want a gold watch. Shit," Lila said, then lapsed
into silence.

Amos stood up and said "Are you the manager?" to
the dainty little man who followed the pudgy blinking
salesgirl down the stairs.

The salesgirl nodded 'yes' to Amos' question.

"Have you told him everything?" Amos asked her,
helping Lila up.

"Yes." The left eye never stopped moving.

"What did he say?"

"He said he cannot understand why, if you didn't take
the watch, you won't open your wife's purse."

"Tell him I'm waiting for an apology."

"*Vuole una scusa.*"

"*Ma, pensa che sia matto? È un ladro?*"

"Non, credo, ma con gli americani non si sa mai."

"I caught something about Americans," Amos said. "What were you saying?"

"I said you are very strange people and I do not understand you."

"Can't we just forget all this?" Lila said. "Please," and she took her purse back from her husband, tucked it under her arm.

"In cases like this," the salesgirl said, "sometimes the police are useful."

"Police!" Amos looked around the empty store. "We came in here to buy watches. Look," and he brought out his wallet, removing a sheaf of traveler's checks. "Have him count this. What the hell would we want to steal a watch for when we can pay for it? Hell, tell him I wrote 'Francie.' "

The salesgirl turned to the manager. *"Dice che ha scritto 'Francie.' "*

"Ma chi e questo 'Francie'? Di che cosa parla?"

"He says he does not know who is this Francie of yours and what are you talking about?" The left eye never moved faster.

"The song, my God, the song, everybody knows 'Francie,' " Amos said and he suddenly burst madly into the opening chorus, waving his arms, belting his heart out in the empty store for the pudgy salesgirl and the tall guard and the dainty manager who thought he was a thief. "Ask him if he hasn't heard it. I wrote it. I'm respectable for chrissakes. Tell him that."

"Vuole che Lei sappia che lui sia un uomo per bene," the girl told the manager.

121

"*Ma un orologio e proprio sparito?*" the manager called to the guard.

"*Li ho contati me stresso. Due volte,*" the guard answered.

"*Allora contiamo una terza volta,*" the manager said and he and the guard set to it.

"They will count the watches again," the girl said, so Amos moved to the counter watching closely as the manager and the guard fingered the watches, so he wasn't paying much attention when Lila and the girl came over, or when Lila dropped to her knees, or, a moment after that, when Lila started saying "Look, look," over and over. The girl dropped to her knees then, rising quickly saying "Oh . . . oh . . . I'm terribly sorry . . . terribly sorry," the unaccounted-for watch in her hands, suddenly accounted for now. "It must have fallen," she said to Amos. "It was half hidden. I'm . . . terribly sorry." The manager was watching her and she told him, "*L'orologio ha caduto. Nessumo l'ha visto. Era mezzo mascosto del tappeto. Sono innocenti.*"

The manager put a dainty hand to his face. "*Mi dispiace moltissimo,*" he said.

"He is terribly sorry too," the salesgirl said, her left hand covering her eye.

"He apologizes?" Amos asked.

"He definitely apologizes."

"He's full of regret?"

"Yes, yes."

"He admits we're not thieves?"

"We do not have things like this happen to us. We are one of the two best stores in Rome."

"Fine," Amos said. "Then would you please sell my wife a watch."

"Amos—no—"

"Come on, Lila; what else can happen?"

"No I said!" Lila cried, whirling and suddenly gone from the store, and Amos, stunned, followed her frantically into the crowded Rome night thinking what a golden idea it had been in the beginning, to buy her a watch, what a good and sweet thing, and look what had happened to it now, and wasn't it lucky he hadn't been current during Calvary because if he had, and he'd somehow got the guts to shinny up the cross with a cup of something cool to help the poor Bastard, it would probably have turned out to be salt water that he'd cradled in his hands.

iii

For the city of Venice, with all his romantic soul, Amos had only one wish: that it should sink. That really wasn't being fair, he realized: the buildings themselves were glorious. But the canals did stink, the gondoliers did cheat, his fellow visitors made a clear view of anything but the backs of their heads impossible, and the natives, bred on pasta and tourism, kept reaching out from doorways, grabbing your elbow, beseeching you to for God's sakes come to the glass factory, and in all other ways conceivable, nickel-and-dimed you to death.

On top of all that, you couldn't get to Venice. Not easily anyway. Amos had taken an early flight from Rome, but the next plane wasn't for several hours, which meant that after he'd checked into the Gritti Palace, the wait for Lila was intolerable. He sat in his room awhile, staring glumly at the Grand Canal, trying to figure just what to say to Lila when she got there. Because, he had decided, the time had come for them to talk, honestly for once, about their 'situation' and how could they go about taming it, civilizing it, pacifying it, so that the dove of peace might fly triumphant.

He left his room eventually, getting very precise instructions from the concierge below on how to reach the

Piazza San Marco. The concierge repeated the instructions twice, without being asked, because, he told Amos, Venice was the hardest city in the world to find your way around although, he admitted, he had never been to Tokyo.

Amos, with only one or two minor mishaps, made the Piazza, and as he approached it, he could actually feel his heart, because Venice was the most romantic city in the world and the Piazza was the most romantic part of it and he figured that somehow, once he and Lila walked hand in hand through it in the moonlight, their troubles might snap, or start to at least, but when he reached the Piazza he was crushed because all their guidebooks talked of its tranquillity, whereas Amos, staring around, was reminded of what it was like trying to get a hot dog beneath the stands of Palmer stadium at halftime of a Princeton-Yale game. As he moved across the blazing square, children shrieked and hawkers hawked and pigeons flapped and people kept bumping him and half a dozen bands played on and on. It was not a spot conducive to reducing Lila's soul to jelly, Amos decided, especially since the bands played 'Francie' just enough off-key but loud, again and again and again.

Still he wandered around the place for hours, staring at all the tourist-trap stores that lined the square, peddling junk in infinite variety, and he took a seat in the shade as far as he could from a band, downing a bottle of sparkling mineral water as he read yesterday's copy of the Paris *Herald Tribune* and Willie wasn't doing so good, at least no homers, and Amos quickly decided that that was not an omen. He stayed in the square until he thought Lila's plane might be about landed and then did his best to get back to the hotel, which he did, finally, cursing the couple of wrong turns he took. When he reached the room, Lila was already unpacking.

He went up and hugged her. "Cry much on the plane?"

She shook her head. "Only while we were in the air."

"That's something," Amos said. "Like the hotel?"

"It's kind of understaffed, wouldn't you say?"

Amos nodded. "Earlier I had to open the elevator door myself. Shocking."

"How's the city? It looks kind of breath-taking. Is San Marco as beautiful as they say?"

"Haven't been there yet," Amos answered. "I thought we ought to see it for the first time together."

"Where've you been then?"

"Just now you mean?" Amos shrugged. "Window-shopping."

Lila looked at him. "That's very considerate, Amos, waiting for me. Thank you."

Amos made a smile.

"Let me just hang up a few things and we'll scoot."

"Deal."

Lila whisked through the rest of her luggage, slapping at a few dresses as she hung them up, hopefully driving the wrinkles away. Leaving the rest of her debris in the suitcase, she nodded to Amos and they left the hotel. "I found out which way it is," Amos said. "Stay close. This place is a maze," and he led her along, pausing a few times when he didn't have to to get his bearings and when they were near the piazza he said, "It's got to be right up thataway."

"God I'm excited."

"Me too," Amos agreed, taking her hand, and together they moved toward the sound. At the edge of the square, they stopped a moment. "It's just like I imagined," Lila said. "Oh Amos, don't you love it?"

Amos nodded.

"And listen, they're playing 'Francie.' "

Amos smiled. "Even in Venice."

"And look at the pigeons. Aren't they something?"

"I feel like I'm in a movie," Amos said, thinking, 'You're disappointed too, so why can't we both say so?' "I think it's about as beautiful as any place I've ever seen."

"Like they say, the words from my mouth." She moved on ahead of him, ploughing as best she could through the noisy crowd. All around them, pigeons flapped.

"Talk about colorful," Amos said.

"Do you think we could sit down at one of the cafés and just take it all in?"

Amos nodded. "I don't think there's any law against it." He led her to a table, first shooing away a cluster of pigeons, and they sat in the broiling sun, quietly, until Amos ordered a large bottle of mineral water, sparkling, and two glasses.

"Hey I've been thinking," Lila said, once their order arrived and Amos had paid.

"To your health," Amos said, raising his glass of mineral water. They toasted and drank the cool liquid and the noise around them was terrifying, but Amos heard every word when Lila said, "I think we should try a separation."

"Thank God," Amos told her. "I've been eating myself alive trying to figure how to say the same thing."

Lila sighed and reached out, taking his hand. "I thought we were in for a blisterer on this."

"Sometimes we're on the same wavelength," Amos said.

"It's just the only thing," Lila went on. "On the plane today, it came to me. A separation really seems like the answer for now. We'll be in the same city, you can still see Jessica when you want."

"And we'll both date, right? I think that's the sensible way. And if we miss each other, swell; if we don't, a divorce won't come as anything sudden."

"That's just the way I had it figured."

"I'll move out of the apartment—I think it'd be easier on Jeremiah if she could keep her same surroundings— and then we'll just wing it and see."

"You know something, Amos? We're really talking to each other. That's always been one of our troubles. We haven't communicated as well as some people."

"I always thought we talked great with each other."

"Well we talked, Amos; no doubt about our being verbal—it's just that I haven't always felt you've been as honest with me as now."

"We must be slipping into maturity," Amos said, standing. "Let's hit the hotel. It's a little warmish here." He started moving through the square, Lila alongside. Pigeons swarmed through the air, and Amos, drenched and steaming in his dark grey Dacron from Brooks thought that he had at last reached it, the bottom of the pit, until from the pale blue Venetian sky, a pigeon unloaded on his left shoulder.

Amos stared up at the pigeon. "Just give the news, please," he said.

As they made the final turn left toward the Gritti, Lila broke the silence with, "I thought you were really wonderful. About the separation I mean."

"Shucks, ma'am, twarn't nothin," Amos replied, continuing to swipe with his handkerchief at the remains on his left shoulder. "What does 'twarn't' mean do you think? They're always saying that in Westerns. 'Twarn't,' " and he kept on babbling away because he wasn't entirely sure what he would do with silence right then. "Venice is really the place, you know?" he said, launching into an extolling of virtues which carried them close to the Gritti when he stopped, cold, because he saw a Venetian child then, all dressed in bright colors, who resembled no one so much as she did Edward G. Robinson and he punched Lila and gestured. "Think you could get her picture? You carrying the Minox?"

"It's a fantastic resemblance," Lila said. "I wonder if she'd mind if I took a close-up. Where's your phrase book? See if it says 'Can I take your picture?' "

Amos opened his Italian guide and began thumbing through, all the time glancing at the Venetian child, thankful that Lila saw the resemblance too, because if she hadn't he would have known his mind had gone, finally and irrevocably, and for the rest of his life he would be condemned to seeing tiny Edward G. Robinsons because his own child had been so ruthlessly ripped away from him. "This phrase book is great if you want to ask 'Is there a good hotel in Gubbio?' for chrissakes." He snapped it shut and stuffed it back into his pocket. "I'll do it in sign language." He approached the Venetian child and said, *"Scusi,* but pictoro? Picture? Snappashotta? You?" and he pointed his finger at the child, smiling as winningly as he could.

"I'm the leader," the child said, suddenly running into his arms, and the next thing Amos heard was Lila shrieking with unabashed delight, *"Mother!!!"* as Jessica Rowan herself stepped coolly out from behind the closest corner.

At the age of forty-nine, Jessica Rowan looked at least ten years younger in the face, twenty in the figure, and, as Amos once informed Lila, had handled in her lifetime more balls than Warren Spahn, an admittedly bad joke for the twin reasons that it was neither funny nor true. Jessica didn't *give* charity affairs, she *attended* them. She was one of those ladies who always got their picture in the paper the day after the Metropolitan opened and it was nearly impossible, at least in Manhattan, to have *any* kind of *do* at all without inviting Jessica. She glittered little on the international scene, though, since she wasn't really quite rich enough and when she remarried, which she did once, not successfully, her second spouse wasn't quite significant enough, being nothing more than a close relation to the Du Ponts. What Jessica really was, Amos had again informed Lila, was a road company Jackie Kennedy.

"Whatever are you doing here?" Lila squealed.

"Well after our phone call," her mother replied, "I just thought wouldn't it be fun to pop in and surprise little Jessie here, and then I thought, when I got to London, why not go whole hog and surprise you too. So here we are. I just bought her the clothes. Glad to see me?"

Lila beamed. "Do you have to ask?"

"That rotten bitch!"

Amos lay on the bed in their hotel room, reflecting that if comedy was based on incongruity, then his wife was comic now as she sat across the room from him, clad in her Wragge suit, going rapidly through guidebook after guidebook, her rarely worn horn-rims in place, the picture of tranquil-blonde-young-American-intellectuality, while from her mouth poured venom.

"Oh that rotten, stinking—"

"Surely you can't be referring to your mum?"

"Shut up, just shut up, oh that lousy bitch, coming here."

"They're just down the hall y'know. Either tone it down or pitch it up and we'll dance to it."

Lila tossed one guidebook aside, grabbed up another. "You know why she's here, don't you? You know why she just had to come. She's saying 'I told you so' to me about marrying you."

"The best thing about our separating is I get to leave her too."

Lila flipped through the pages of the guidebook. "She knew in Rome after the phone call something was wrong so she just had to be here. Our final pffft she just had to see."

"Listen," Amos said, flopping toward the wall. "If it makes your life any easier, I'll try stomaching you a while longer." He waited for a reply until none came and Lila was crying out, "I knew it! I knew it was here someplace!" and then Amos turned, watching his wife parade the room, book held high.

"I knew I'd find it, Amos. Back in New York when you first said let's go to Europe and I bought these guide-books and was taxiing home I remembered something thumbing through and now I've got it. It's here. The Ghetto, Amos! I'll take her to the Ghetto! I'll take that rotten bitch to the Ghetto tonight as a surprise!"

Amos lay quietly back on the bed, watching her move.

"Is that brilliant, Amos? Yes? You're being awfully quiet. Is that a fantastic idea? You bet it is. Say so, damn you."

Very quietly, Amos said, "You're going to take your mother to a ghetto, is that the gist of what you're saying?"

"Not *a* ghetto, for chrissakes—listen to me when I talk —*the* Ghetto. The first stinking ghetto in the history of the world—it's right here in Venice—I'll take her there —only I won't tell her where it is we're going—it's a surprise I'll tell her—her own very special one—Mother loves surprises."

Amos shut his eyes.

"Well?" Lila said.

"That'll really fix her, Lila old kid. Yes sir, you've got a real head on your shoulders. I mean, hats off."

"I sense a certain sarcasm."

"Well Jesus, what's she supposed to do, break into little pieces when you tell her it's the Ghetto?"

"You don't have to shout—"

"Who the hell's shouting?—I'm just trying to say who the hell's gonna care about going to the Ghetto or not?"

"What's eating you all of a sudden?"

"You have to shout sometimes to get through to the lower forms of animal life—nothing'll happen, don't you get that? She won't care. She'll just think it's a bad joke—"

"She'll know she's the butt of it, won't she, buster? She'll gather that much, wouldn't you say? Well that's plenty, don't you think?"

"I think it's one of the stupidest goddam things you've ever thought of and believe me, you've thought of some pretty goddamned stupid things—"

"Now you're getting violent—"

"Nobody's violent! You're the one that's violent! I'm just telling you it would be disaster, that's all."

"Mother loves disasters," Lila said.

"Lila, what *is* your surprise," Mrs. Rowan was saying. "I cannot stand the suspense another minute."

"Have to," Lila answered, smiling out at the Grand Canal. It was evening, and they were dining late on the terrace of the Gritti, the three of them, Jessica having been put to bed, complete with sitter, in Mrs. Rowan's suite, over an hour before. "Now it's my secret, Mother, and it's all been taken care of. So no more questions."

"Amos, do you know what it is?"

Amos shook his head, even though he knew Mrs. Rowan didn't believe him. He tugged and straightened the sleeves of his fresh-pressed khaki suit. "I'm sure it'll be a lot of fun though," he said, and he did his best to duplicate his wife's smile, in spite of the fact that his back was killing him.

"Is something the matter, Amos?" Mrs. Rowan said.

"No. Nothing. Just my back kicking up."

"Oh you and your back," Lila said.

"It hurts, Lila, I can't help it."

"There's nothing wrong with your back."

"How much you wanna bet, Lila? I'll get every doctor in New York to look at my X rays and I'll bet anything you say they all tell you I've got disc trouble."

"Bet-bet-bet—you're like a two-year-old."

"You do sound childish, Amos. I'm not taking Lila's side, you understand. But really, can't we act like adults? Now let's just drink our coffee and you can tell me all about Rome."

"We loved it," Amos said. "Except for when this place thought we'd stolen a watch. I was thinking of buying Lila a watch and—"

"Not a gold watch, was it?"

"Yes, as a matter of fact," Amos began. "See, this very fancy spot miscounted and—"

"Lila, do you remember your father and the gold watch?"

Lila shook her head. "No, what happened, tell me."

"It was nothing, really. He said he'd buy you one and then he didn't have the money. He felt very embarrassed about it as I remember. Of course, he should have."

"Doesn't ring a bell," Lila said. "Go on. What happened then?"

"Nothing, that's all," Mrs. Rowan said.

"I really hope you like my surprise," Lila said, looking at her mother.

Mrs. Rowan signaled for more coffee. "I'm sinfully ignorant of Rome, really. Venice, of couse, I'm more familiar with. Though I've never been here quite this time of year before. Amos?"

"Yes, Jessica?"

"Next time you ought to come here in September. All the fairies from all over Europe come here then. All the important ones, I should say. The Venetians even have a name for them: *Settemberini*, they're called. You really ought to be here for it, Amos."

"What the hell's that supposed to mean," Amos said.

Mrs. Rowan smiled. "Oh surely I wasn't insinuating anything. I only meant that you'd enjoy it because so many of them are in the theatre. That is your line of work, after all. You are an artist."

Lila stood then. "Shall we?"

Amos stood too, carefully, so as not to send his back into spasm.

"Where are we going?" Mrs. Rowan wanted to know.

"My treat," Lila said. "My surprise. Everything's been taken care of. Come on."

They left the Gritti and walked around the corner and there, at the canal, a gondola waited. They all got in and the gondolier pushed off, and for a while they stayed on the Grand Canal. Amos began massaging his back, hoping he had enough money with him to cover any contingency, because he had always distrusted water and from the first moment he got to town he'd taken his passport wallet and traveler's checks and hidden them in his dresser drawer because if a gondola tipped over and you had to swim for it and you lost your passport and money, what would you do then?

"Hoi," the gondolier cried, and slowly they drifted from the Grand Canal into a smaller artery. Amos pressed his thumb knuckle into the small of his back, easing his pain as he tried very hard to concentrate on the beauty of the ancient buildings gliding by.

"Hoi," the gondolier cried again, just before another turn, and this time there was an answering cry, "Hoi," from the darkness ahead of them and another gondola slipped briefly into view.

"I'm terribly excited," Mrs. Rowan said.

Amos said nothing, continuing to press hard with his thumb knuckle, all the time knowing that somehow, in some terrible unknown way, everything was slowly building to climax, which confused him because he and Lila had had their climax already, that afternoon, in the pigeon-infested square.

"Hoi," the gondolier cried at the next turning. "Hoi," again as the craft made its steady way. The canals were very narrow now and Amos jumped at the sight of a rat skittering along the edge of a building just above the waterline, and he wondered what he would do if the rat jumped into the gondola, would the gondolier take care of it or would he have to somehow rise to the terrible occasion and grapple with the filthy thing in the darkness, all the while being careful not to tip the boat and drown them all in the scum of the canal?

The rat disappeared into an ancient doorway and Amos sighed, happy for just a moment before a tiny rage seized him because there it had been again, his goddam paranoia, and chances are it wouldn't have worked anyway, his marriage, he would never have been able to please a girl like Lila enough, but the crazy way he got worked up over things sure hadn't helped things any.

". . . hoi . . ."

". . . hoi . . ."

They had been gone for a long time now, longer than Amos thought possible in a town no bigger than Venice, and no one was talking. There was nothing, no sound at all, except the slip of the oar into the water and the turning cries of the gondolier.

". . . hoi . . ."

". . . hoi . . ."

Amos glanced at his wife, sitting straight and still, and then at the bitch of all the world, turning her coifed head from side to side, trying to guess where they were going, and suddenly it seemed to Amos like a perfect symbolic end-of-marriage thing that he was doing, going to visit with some stinking anti-Semite the place where, five hundred years before, they first started herding up the Jews.

The gondola stopped.

From behind them, the gondolier said something in Italian and Amos watched as the man gestured and Lila nodded. Then Lila stood and stepped from the craft, Jessica following. Finally Amos, back throbbing, made his careful way to safety. The gondolier tied up his boat and gesturing again for them to follow, started walking quickly away.

Mrs. Rowan hurried up to him saying, "Tell me where we're going."

"He doesn't *capisco*," Lila told her mother.

"Amos, you tell me."

"I don't know," Amos said.

The gondolier continued on his way, the three of them doing their best to follow. As they turned and twisted along the narrow streets, Amos, in the rear, limping now, remembered something he had once heard a wonderful old Scot say about the salmon country of his birth: 'It's so wild, that if you get lost, you just die.' Amos hurried then, catching up to Lila, walking close beside her, wondering what would happen if the gondolier, who seemed young enough, suddenly keeled over because you could never tell about coronaries, and would he, Amos, be able to take command and find his way back to the gondola and once there, to the Grand Canal, and *there it was again! the craziness!* It had driven a stake into the heart of his marriage and it tormented him still and Amos wanted desperately to drive his thumb knuckle straight through his spine except he needed his hands more to play a few tunes on his kneecaps but he couldn't reach down that far without definitely throwing himself into absolute spasm and then the gondolier stopped, pointing.

They were there.

Amos stared around, disappointed. It wasn't much of anything. Just a bunch of old ugly buildings, tall tenements really, surrounding an old ugly square, which was empty except for a few old ugly people sitting around in the far darkness. Lila signaled for the gondolier to wait and then, arm in arm with her mother, she began walking forward. Amos followed silently behind, stopping when they stopped, in the very center of the square. Lila let her mother go then and slowly began to pivot, arms held wide, a blonde ingénue in the moonlight. "Well?" she said.

"It's lovely," Mrs. Rowan said.

Lila stopped suddenly. "You don't like it."

"I said it was lovely."

"But you didn't mean it. I know you, Mother. I can tell when you're disappointed."

"But I'm not."

"Then let's hear a little enthusiasm, Mother."

Amos backed a silent step away, watching them.

"It's just beautiful, Lila."

"You don't mean that either."

"I do though. I think it's one of the prettiest places in all of Venice, but just what is it, Lila?"

"Prettier than San Marco?"

"Yes."

"Prettier than the Grand Canal?"

"Oh much, but just exactly what—"

"You're lying to me. You're just saying all this to make me happy."

"Lila, what is the matter with you? I love it here. I told you. It's glorious."

"More."

"What do you mean, 'More'?"

"I mean I'd like to be able to believe you. I'd like to know you mean it."

"What more is there? Lovely, beautiful, glorious, quiet, out of the way—"

"—but not too much out of the way," Lila cut in quickly.

"Oh no," Mrs. Rowan said. "Just the right amount. Why are you acting like this? Where are we, Lila?"

"We're in my surprise."

"I know that, dear. But however did you find it?"

"It was easy."

"Are you being purposely obscure or am I being stupid?"

"It was in the guidebooks under G, Mother."

Mrs. Rowan shook her head and stared at her daughter.

Lila began to laugh.

Mrs. Rowan turned to Amos. "I've taken enough teasing now, don't you think? Where are we?"

Amos said nothing.

"Tell me, Amos."

Amos said nothing.

Mrs. Rowan turned back to her daughter. "Surely it can't be all that funny, Lila—"

Lila nodded that it was, and laughed.

"You can stop laughing now."

Lila shook her head.

"Stop your silly laughing!" Mrs. Rowan said, turning on Amos again. "I'm growing quite disenchanted, Amos. Where are we?"

Amos said nothing.

"Tell her," from Lila.

Amos said the word.

Mrs. Rowan repeated it after him, starting to turn slowly around and around, staring at the dark buildings.

Lila laughed louder.

"Well, I'm confused," Mrs. Rowan said then, continuing her turns, her stares. "I simply do not understand. You brought me to the Ghetto, Lila. Fine. Now please tell me why. Was I supposed to turn into a pumpkin?" but when Lila wouldn't stop her laughing, Mrs. Rowan turned on Amos again. "All right, suppose you tell me. I don't catch the joke. Surely I can't be expected to appreciate a joke until I understand it. Explain it to me, Amos; surely this was your brand of humor. Was this supposed to hurt me? Make me mad? It doesn't, you know."

Nothing from Amos.

"It's not worth all this, Amos—now tell me!"

Nothing from Amos.

"Oh come along, Lila," Mrs. Rowan said then. "I'm very disappointed in you, letting Amos influence you this way," and she had taken just a few steps before she whirled around, voice rising with "You always think it's so funny, Amos, people like you. You're just such a wonderful sensitive artist and anything you do is fine because we're all supposed to be so fortunate, the rest of us, having you around brightening our days. Well I'll tell you something—I'll tell you something—"

"Kiss my Jewish ass," Amos said.

Nothing from Mrs. Rowan.

"Only the left cheek actually," Amos went on, "but that counts, doesn't it?" and Mrs. Rowan started to turn away from him but he was on her like a shot shouting "I asked you a question—being half—that counts—doesn't it count?—I mean, what was good enough for Hitler should be good enough for you so answer me!" and he was about to go on, in high gear, because it was out now, out and spoken in the night, and he would have gone on, except that as Mrs. Rowan ripped free of him and started away he saw that his wife was going with her.

Panting, Amos watched them, watched as Lila turned every few steps, turned and stared back at him as if he was a freak, and until she did that he almost cried out 'Lila don't leave me' but fuck her, he didn't need her, he didn't need anybody, not one bloody soul, because he was Amos McCracken and 'Francie' was his song so the *New York Times* would jot him down come judgment day and "Lila don't leave me!"

Lila left him.

"Don't worry you two!" Amos screamed after them. *"As long as there's Halloween you'll never be out of a job!"*

Amos watched them until they were gone. His back hurt like crazy and he wondered if he might be getting a headache, but all in all, he was okay—no. Better than okay; he was fine. Fine and strong and on his own and it was all going to work out, because he'd get to see the kid a couple of times a week and they'd have great times together, nothing but great times, and he'd undo all the damage done by her mother the days he wasn't around. And the kid would report on what a shriveled-up bitch her mother was turning into—no. Lila was too desirable to shrivel so soon. Probably she'd remarry. Some bare-brained half-ass of a Wall Street jerk and wouldn't that be the match of the century, wouldn't that be perfect—no. Not so perfect because when she remarried that meant there'd be two daddies in the family and that wasn't so good if you were who he was because in the long run, you lost, you were extra, not needed, so you had to lose, and Amos suddenly saw her on the phone, fifteen and beautiful, his little Jasmine, all resemblance to Edward G. Robinson gone, talking to some rich fucking freshman from Princeton about how she couldn't see him this Sunday because that was the one day each month she had to spend with her, you should pardon the expression, father, and if there was a bigger drag than him around she'd eat it, because all he did was talk about some crappy song he'd written a thousand years ago, the last thing he'd ever done, the last successful thing anyway, because none of the junk he turned out nowadays reached Broadway any more.

Without a sound, Amos sank down to the stones and lay still, arms stretched out wide, eyes examining the Venetian sky.

"*Sta male Lei? C'è qualcosa che non va?*"

Amos stared up at the old Italian who was suddenly peering anxiously down at him. "I'm fine," Amos said.

The old man touched Amos' head. "*Ha svanito? Ha caduto Lei?*"

"Don't worry yourself, sir. I'm really okay."

The old man tried lifting Amos to his feet. "*Mi lasci aiutar Lei.*"

"Believe me, I'm just fine down here," and he lay flat again.

"C'è qualcosa rotta forse?"

"Everything is all right. Now just will you please leave me alone."

The old man scurried, bent over, away.

Alone again, Amos tried to remember where he'd been before the interruption. Yes. Lila had remarried and Jabez was fifteen and hated him and he hadn't written a song in a decade and suddenly the old man was back pointing down at him again, saying *"Eccolo, eccolo."*

Amos stared up, beginning to feel embarrassed at the way the half-dozen men were looking down at him. "Thanks an awful lot for bothering with me like this," Amos said, "but I'm really fine."

"You're fine?" one of the six said.

Amos nodded.

"Dice che sta bene," the one who knew English said.

"Ma allora perche sta sdraiato sulla terra? È ubriaco?" another man said.

"If you're so fine," the translator said, "he wants to know why you are lying on the stones? Are you drunk?"

"No. I'm a Jew. I belong here."

"We're all Jews," the translator said. "But you don't see us lying on the stones." He turned to the group around him. *"Lui dice che è un ebreo e che dovrebb'essere qua."*

"Matto," one of the old Jews said.

"What does *matto* mean?" Amos wanted to know.

"Crazy," the translator said.

Another old man said, *"Io credo che gli americani divengano più pazzo ogni anno. Ho visto molto più americani pazzi quest'anno che l'anno scorso."*

"He says he thinks the Americans are getting crazier as time goes on. He says he has seen many more crazy Americans this year than last."

"Dillo che non puo stare qua," another old man said. *"Dillo di muoversi."*

"He says you can't stay here. You've got to move."

"Look, I'm just lying here not bothering a living soul so—"

"This is our home. What if the police found you? We don't want you giving our home a bad name."

I'm giving the Ghetto a bad name, Amos thought. I must be the first guy in history to pull that off. Slowly, without a word, he stood and carefully brushed at his clothes. The old men watched him. Amos smiled at them. "I guess maybe an explanation—" he said and then he said, "—you see—" and then, "—this back of mine—" but by that time he was too embarrassed to say any more so he only muttered " 'night" and started walking. Halfway across the square he stopped and turned, but they were still watching him, shaking their ancient heads, muttering to each other, gesturing with withered hands.

Amos left the square, concentrating very hard on remembering how they had gotten to the place, and in just a few minutes he made it to where the gondola had been. It wasn't any more, but he hadn't much expected it to be. Shoving his hands deep into his pockets, Amos began to walk. The concierge had told him what a complicated city Venice was to find your way around, what with canals suddenly ending, streets too, and bridges not being where they ought to be and Amos could only agree. He wandered along, dazed, looking for the least sign of life, turning one way, then another, and when, in a particularly dark street no more than five feet wide, he heard movement in the shadows up ahead of him, he didn't know whether he was going to have the courage to ask directions. But desperate men do desperate things so Amos said "San Marco?" and the figure in the darkness replied *"Non si puo sbagliarla,"* and probably pointed, though Amos could neither see nor understand what he had heard so he just said *"Grazie, grazie,"* and continued on. Later, in more light he saw an old woman who said *"Giri a destra,"* and later, another one, who told him, *"Vada sempre diritto,"* and gradually, as he gathered directions, all the words assumed rhythms in Amos' musical brain. *"Giù di la. Giri a destra. Poi giri alla prima strada a sinistra. Giri a sinistra. Vada sempre diritto."*

Beautiful, Amos thought. Beautiful words in a beautiful tongue and even the pain in his back could not deprive his appreciation of how lovely the sounds were. But as he continued to wander, it crossed his mind that all the directions in the world weren't any good to him now, even if he understood the sounds, because he didn't know what his destination might be, but then he said *stop it half ass!* because his destination had to be the Gritti Palace because that was where his passport was, and there wasn't any point to getting melodramatic again as he had before when he'd lain like a fool on the cool Ghetto stones.

So he began asking for the Grand Canal and eventually, although he thought for a while his back was going in spasm, he found it, and then things were easier, because you could lose the Grand Canal, but not for long, not if you concentrated, and Amos did concentrate, on the Grand Canal and where was it wandering and the same question held for him too, he supposed, where was he wandering now? Because he was thirty and a half years old and everything was shit. No. That was too easy, Marx would have said. The easiest thing, Marx said, was to think everything was wonderful. The second easiest thing was to think everything was shit. The third thing, the hard thing, the only hard and right and proper thing to think was this: to affirm in spite of. So what if a pigeon dive-bombs you; there's always dry cleaning. So what if your wife leaves you, there's always air to breathe. You can breathe air and see sky and so what if it stinks, getting through the day, if you don't like it, there's always the river to breathe, and the reason he and Lila didn't make it through more days was because for them everything was either shit or wonderful and not once did either of them ever think to say—hey!—it's both!—

And so was he. Sure he was crazy. Yes he was impossible. Okay, paranoid too. And sometimes cruel when it crossed his mind that the world might be able to get along without him. And a lousy insomniac. And a miserable companion, especially when there was some tune in his head taunting him because it wouldn't come out. But there were tunes! Real-honest-to-Christ-make-you-wanna-cry-tunes. And someday he was gonna nail the bastards and drag them kicking and screaming out of his skull and then, by Christ—

"Then you're gonna hear something!" Amos cried.

He entered the Gritti Palace. The concierge, frail and omnipotent, nodded at him from behind his desk as Amos crossed the lobby saying, "I'm Amos McCracken and I've got to get out of here."

"Are you all right, Mr. McCracken?" the concierge said.

'Why do you ask that?' Amos was about to reply, but then he caught a glimpse of his khaki suit, and how wrinkled and mussed it was. "You mean on account of I'm dressed this way? I don't blame you for asking. London. That's where my silent keyboard is. Can you get me there?"

The old man nodded. "I'll reserve a space on the afternoon flight."

"I can't wait till afternoon. Isn't there any place else around here with flights to London?"

"There is Milan."

"Terrific. Book me on the first job to Milan and I'll transfer."

"Yes sir. That flight leaves at noon so you'd best leave the hotel by—"

"Wait a sec, please." Amos rubbed his eyes. "Isn't there a Milan train or something that leaves sooner?"

"Yes, Mr. McCracken. But it arrives later."

Amos rubbed his eyes again. "I suppose I could go straight to New York and to heck with the keyboard."

"Are you sure you're all right, Mr. McCracken?"

"Marvelous, yes, only how's this: I'll take a gondola to the railroad station and I'll taxi from there to Milan. That would be good, wouldn't it? I bet it's a beautiful drive."

"You won't be able to see it so well at night, Mr. Mc-Cracken."

Amos leaned heavily down on the desk. "I gotta move is the thing. Can you help me? Please?"

The old head nodded. "I'll get you a gondola. I'll get you a car."

"My wallet and passport are in my room, I'll be right down," and he had turned almost completely away before wheeling back to the wizard. "Would you deliver a message for me too?"

As the objects materialized in his hands, the concierge said, "Pen, paper, envelope."

"She can't read is the thing," and for a moment Amos could feel himself starting to go, but then someone whipped him with *'Cut that you stinking sissy!'* so, very clearly, he said, "Tell her not to believe anything they say about me."

"Tell who, Mr. McCracken? Please let me get you some brandy. Perhaps some American coffee—"

"My girl's who I'm talking about. She's in Mrs. Rowan's suite tonight, just down the hall from our room. But don't tell her what I just told you. Tell her this: tell her it isn't her fault. No. Don't tell her that. Tell her . . . just tell her it would have happened a long time ago except for her. No. Wait. That's not it either. Tell her—hey, I've got it! Just sing 'Twinkle Twinkle Little Star' to her only I'll give you some different lyrics—see,

I'll make up some lyrics and you'll sing them to her in the morning and everything'll be terrific—see, I'm a songwriter so this'll mean a lot to her, more than anything to her . . . 'Twinkle twinkle little star, how I wonder what you are'—those are the words I gotta change—this'll just take a sec—hell, back at Princeton they used to throw songs at me and I'd come right back with new lyrics like a shot . . . I'm not saying they're good lyrics, y'understand, but at least they fit and they make sense and lemme think now, how's this: 'Listen closely little girl.' See, that scans the same as 'Twinkle twinkle little star' so we're off and running and all I need's a rhyme for girl. Twirl, how's that? Stinks. Furl? What does furl have to do with telling her? . . . Curl? —Christ, any stinking hack would use curl and this has got to be a good song. Just once in my life I wanna do something good—hurl?—pearl?—swirl?—what if I use 'child' instead of 'girl'? Think that's any better? I gotta tell her is the thing, she's just gotta know. Mild, wild, filed, piled, tiled, riled, styled, or—or—"

"Mr. McCracken—"

"I need a song for my baby!"

The concierge reached out then, rested a soft hand on Amos' shoulder.

I did that to Nino, Amos thought. I put my hand on his shoulder. After I'd screwed up there too. He shook his head slowly. ". . . all I wanted was a song for my baby . . . how do you like that . . . Amos McCracken and he couldn't come up with a song . . ."

"I'm sorry, Mr. McCracken."

"I must be very tired, do you think? Could I have my key now please? And could you fix up the boat and the car?"

The old man nodded, reached for the key.

Amos took it, went to the elevator, leaned against the wall while it rode him, eyes closed, to his floor. When he stepped out into the corridor he opened his eyes and halfway along was the door to Mrs. Rowan's suite. As he approached it Amos wondered if he was up to taking the bull by the horns and asking Jasmine flat out—give her her choice: either spend the rest of her life with watchamacallit or leave with him, leave now, just go, and have nothing but fun forever. Put it straight to her. It was her life, for God's sake, so why shouldn't she at least have a little say in which direction it was going and *wait a minute—*

She's a kid. A kid! Quit with that craziness. How can you expect a kid to know what to do with her life? And how could you think you could straighten her out by writing a parody to 'Twinkle Twinkle Little Star' for some stranger to sing her in the morning?

She's four years old . . . it's the middle of the night . . . let her sleep . . .

Amos continued wearily on past Mrs. Rowan's door to his own. He let himself in and went quietly to the drawer where he'd left his passport and wallet. He found them quickly, stuffed them into the proper pockets, then turned again for the door, facing only briefly the feminine lump on the bed. He couldn't hear her breathing so maybe she was awake too, and maybe her eyes were also open, watching his moves, which made them wary adversaries, familiar with each other's feints, opponents in some ornate jungle, gladiators, veterans of infinite tussles and scuffles and battles and wars who somehow miraculously survived to fight again and again and—no. There was nothing in the least miraculous about them. They were just a half-hebe and a boobless bitch who hadn't hit it off.

He had started for the door when she said, "Amos listen," and his reply was just "Let's give it a rest, Lila," because that was the best thing to do, and to her "No, listen to me," he only said, "I'm awful tired, Lila, you must be tired too," but as she went on to "I stole the watch, Amos," he came back with, "I'll be in New York," and by the time she'd said, "I stole it but when they found out I dropped it on the floor," he was already to the door, telling her, "I'll probably be at some hotel, someone'll let you know where—"

"Amos this one time please listen—"

"I am, I am, so you stole the watch," he said, and then he said, "You did?" and after that, softly, he said nothing at all, because what she said meant she was standing at the door and knocking, and Amos at last heard her voice, and opened the door, and came into her, erect and joyous, their imperfect bodies rocking together, touching, he hoped, at least temporarily, and as he rode the splendid creature writhing and falling joyously beneath him, Amos wondered if it might be for more than temporarily, maybe permanent. He wondered for a moment longer, and then the thought was gone. He had, in the